Praise for the **DEAD IS** *Series*

"Fans who mourn the loss of TV's *Veronica Mars* are in for a treat as Perez delivers a wisecracking, boy-lusting, determined sleuth of a high school protagonist. . . . This quick, lighter-than-air spoof of the undead, cheerleaders and popularity is pure pleasure."
—*Publishers Weekly*

"Sassy, romantic, and spooky-fun!"
—Cynthia Leitich Smith, author of *Tantalize*

"A hit. . . . Grabbed me with the first page and didn't let go."
—Julie Kenner, author of
The Good Ghouls' Guide to Getting Even

"Snarky sisters with psychic powers; secret cabals of vamps and werewolves; missing parental(s); and lots of mysteries yet unsolved. Nightshade is my kinda town. . . . Can't wait to hang there again ASAP!"   —Nancy Holder, author of *Pretty Little Devils*

"A fun ride from start to finish. Perez's smart and sassy style soars."—Mary E. Pearson, author of *The Adoration of Jenna Fox*

"Psy-gn me up for more of Daisy and her psychic sisters. Hot romances, cold-hearted, soul-sucking vampires, and cheerleaders dragging roll-around coffins. What's not to love?"
—Gail Giles, author of *Dead Girls Don't Write Letters*

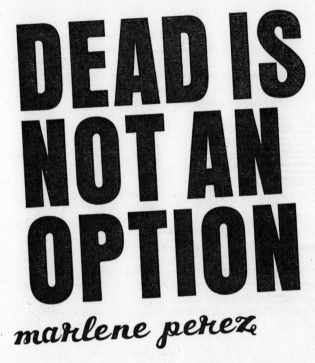

DEAD IS NOT AN OPTION

marlene perez

𝒢 RAPHIA

HOUGHTON MIFFLIN HARCOURT

Boston New York 2011

Copyright © 2011 by Marlene Perez

www.hmhbooks.com

The text of this book is set in Adobe Jenson.

Library of Congress Cataloging-in-Publication Data
Perez, Marlene.
Dead is not an option / Marlene Perez.
p. cm.
Summary: In the spring of her senior year, psychic sleuth Daisy Giordano worries
about getting into a college near her boyfriend, Ryan, but must also investigate and try
to resolve a conflict between vampires and shapeshifters that threatens to cancel prom.
[1. Supernatural—Fiction.   2. Psychic ability—Fiction.   3. High schools—Fiction.
4. Schools—Fiction.   5. Interpersonal relations—Fiction.   6. Sisters—Fiction.]   I. Title.
PZ7.P4258Ddn   2011
[Fic]—dc22   2010027407
ISBN 978-0-547-34593-2

Printed in the United States of America
DOM 10 9 8 7 6 5 4 3 2
4500296925

To the members of the writers' dorm.
Save a spot for me!

DEAD IS NOT AN OPTION

CHAPTER ONE

I was haunting the mailbox. It was already late March and I should have been receiving an acceptance letter anytime, at least that's what I hoped. I had applied to three colleges, but UC Nightshade was my first choice.

It might seem weird to want to stay in the same small town where I'd always lived, but my father, through no fault of his own, had been away from the family and hadn't been back home that long. I couldn't bear to disappoint him by leaving.

Besides, my two older sisters already went to UC Nightshade, so I'd have the benefit of their advice. And more important, my boyfriend, Ryan, was applying to UC Nightshade too.

On my way home from school I spotted someone in a blue uniform standing in front of our mailbox. The postal carrier! But when I rushed up I was surprised to see it wasn't our usual carrier. Instead it was a strange woman with light brown hair who was standing with one hand in our mailbox.

"Where's Mr. Johansson?" I asked. He'd been our mail carrier for years.

The woman turned, startled, and I noticed a purple birthmark on her face.

"Vacation," she mumbled, and hurried off.

I was disappointed to find the mailbox empty. The anticipation was going to kill me. My whole family had noticed my frequent trips to the mailbox, and Poppy sometimes messed with me by hiding the mail.

Mom's car was in the driveway, which meant she was home already. I walked through the front door and into the hallway.

"Daisy, the mail's on the kitchen counter," Mom called from upstairs. It was unusual to find her home before me on a weekday. It must be a slow day for crime. Mom was a psychic investigator, and she helped local law enforcement agencies with their cases. It made life interesting, since Nightshade's chief of police was the father of my boyfriend.

Ryan and I seemed to have inherited their taste for crime solving, since with his help I'd solved several crimes in Nightshade. You know what they say: The couple that solves crimes together stays together. Well, they don't really say that, but they should.

I thumbed quickly through the pile of mail. Bills, junk mail, and a thick envelope for my father, but there wasn't anything for me.

"Mr. Johansson says hello," Mom continued.

"The mailman? I thought he was on vacation," I said.

"What did you say?" Mom hollered.

"Never mind," I replied.

Just then, my cell buzzed. It was Ryan. "Did you get anything yet?" he asked.

"Nothing. You?"

There was silence on the other end of the phone for a moment. "Nothing," he eventually replied.

I sighed.

"Cheer up," he said. "They'll be here soon."

"I'm getting tired of waiting," I said.

"Me too," Ryan admitted.

The unspoken tension between us was caused by one question: What would happen between us if we ended up at different colleges?

Not to mention that my boyfriend was a werewolf, which might be difficult to hide at the dorms. Hiding my psychic abilities would be comparatively easy. The existence of paranormals was starting to be known and accepted in Nightshade, but not everyone in the world had that attitude.

The thought sent me into such a deep funk that I almost missed Ryan's invitation.

"Do you want to do something tonight?" he asked.

"I have to work," I said.

"How about Friday? We'll make it a special date." I was flattered by his insistence.

"Of course," I replied. "What do you have in mind?"

"I just want to see you," he said. "You've been so busy lately."

I'd been busy, it was true, but I also had been avoiding him, using work as an excuse. Everyone said that long-distance relationships never worked. I didn't want to get even closer to Ryan only to break up when we left for separate colleges, or later, when distance took its toll. If we both ended up at UC Nightshade, our relationship stood a chance.

I missed him, though, and couldn't resist temptation.

"I'll make you dinner," I offered. "Everyone will be out of the house."

At least, I was pretty sure they would be. Rose would be out with her boyfriend, Nicholas Bone, and Poppy had a date. She'd been out with her new guy, Liam, almost every night.

Even my parents would be out attending some faculty function at UC Nightshade, where my dad now taught part-time.

"Why don't we go out to dinner?" Ryan asked. "There's something I wanted to talk to you about."

Why can't he talk to me at home? "Sure," I said. "Slim's?"

"I was thinking maybe dinner at Wilder's," Ryan replied.

Wilder's? That was a special-occasion restaurant, not the kind of place we normally went on date night. I once had a few cooking lessons from their former chef, although the lessons were more like unpaid labor than a learning experience.

"Okay," I said after a long pause, "but I thought you were saving money for college."

"You're worth the splurge," Ryan said. "I'll make a reservation for seven."

We hung up after I realized I needed to be at work in half an hour. Business had picked up at Slim's Diner, so I'd been working a lot, which was helping with my college fund. If I got into a college, that is.

I went to talk to my sister Poppy about using the car that night. Both Rose and Poppy still lived at home while they attended UC Nightshade. My parents were ecstatic at the idea of me doing the same. Poppy was on the phone, as usual, but she broke off her conversation to stare at me.

"What?" she said. "I'm on the phone."

"Can I have the car tonight?" I asked.

"Sure," she said. "My date is picking me up here." She'd been awfully mysterious about Liam. We'd met him at an event on Halloween, but she hadn't brought him home and didn't talk about him at all to us, which was definitely not like Poppy.

I drove to work, still wondering what Ryan wanted to talk to me about.

Once there, I went in search of my boss. Slim's had red leather booths, the best cinnamon rolls in the county, and a prophetic jukebox. Not your average diner at all. And the owner and his sister were far from average, as well. The head waitress, Flo, was on her cell phone, in the middle of a very giggly conversation. Probably with her boyfriend. I decided not to interrupt.

There was no sign of Slim, but since he was invisible, there never was. I went in search of him to see what he needed me to do first. I waited tables or helped out in the kitchen, depending on the day.

The kitchen looked empty, but I knew enough to double-check.

"Slim?" I said into the air.

"Hi, Daisy," a voice said.

"Where do you need me tonight?" I asked.

"I've got the dinner menu under control," he said. "Why don't you help Flo?"

Flo was still giggling into her cell phone, so I grabbed some quarters and went to say hello to Lil, the jukebox. She'd given me a ton of clues during my investigations. A few months ago, I'd discovered that there was a soul trapped in there. I'd promised to help her escape her jukebox prison, but so far, I hadn't found a way to do so. I wasn't ready to give up yet, though.

I punched in a few random selections and waited. Nothing. Lil was miffed, and I didn't blame her.

"I'm working on it, I swear," I said. "But Circe took her show on the road and hasn't stepped foot in Nightshade since we found out." What we'd found out was that sorceress and

6

celebrity chef Circe Silvertongue was responsible for trapping Lil in the jukebox and turning her fiancé into a pig.

"A Little Less Conversation" by Elvis Presley came on. Lil was getting impatient.

"Message received," I told her. "A little more action it is. I'll try to figure out what our next step is."

Lil responded with "Inspiration Information" by Sharon Jones and the Dap-Kings and then went silent.

My friends Samantha Devereax and Sean Walsh walked in and sat down at one of the smaller booths. I went over to say hi.

"What are you two doing here tonight?" I said. "You're all dressed up."

Samantha looked gorgeous. She wore a minidress with an itty-bitty cardigan thrown over it. She had her hair piled high and wore long sparkly earrings.

"We're celebrating," Samantha said. "Sean signed his letter of intent."

"Congratulations," I replied. "But what's a letter of intent?"

It wasn't my imagination that they exchanged a meaningful glance.

"Intent to play," Samantha said. "Sean's going to play college baseball with the University of California, Irvine."

Letter of intent? Shouldn't Ryan be signing one of those letter thingies?

7

"I think Slim has some sparkling cider in the back," I said, "left over from Nightshade's anniversary party. I'll bring some out."

"That would be fabulous," Samantha said.

Samantha wasn't angsting like the rest of us. She already knew where she was going—UC Nightshade, where her dad was a big-deal professor. Where my father used to be a big-deal professor and now was a part-time instructor. Big difference. He had a lot more time on his hands now. Maybe that was why nowadays getting the mail was the highlight of his day.

My dad didn't seem to mind that Mr. Devereaux's book was doing very well, even though it was based on research he had done with my dad. But Mr. Devereaux didn't have much money after a pricey divorce from Sam's mom.

"Slim, is it okay if I comp some of that sparkling cider we still have in the cooler? Sam and Sean are celebrating," I said. I explained the occasion, just in case he thought I was trying to score freebies for my friends without a good reason.

"Of course," he said. "And I'll whip up some special appetizers on the house."

"Thanks, Slim," I said. "I'm going to borrow one of the linen tablecloths and some candles, too." We used those on the rare times Slim catered an event.

I knew Sam and Sean were dining at Slim's instead of somewhere fancier in order to save money. But there wasn't any reason I couldn't make their celebration extra special.

Five minutes later, the cider was chilling in a fancy silver bucket, the linen tablecloth hid the scarred tabletop, and Samantha and Sean were gazing into each other's eyes. They were too love struck to even notice when I brought out their appetizers. Mission accomplished.

Lil even cooperated. She broke into a series of slow, romantic love songs. The diner slowly emptied out, but Sam and Sean lingered over their dinner.

Flo was sitting on her favorite stool at the counter, eyeing the clock.

"Why don't you go?" I said. "I'll lock up."

"Are you sure?" Flo asked, but she was already pulling on her jacket.

"Sure, go ahead," I said.

After she left, I stuck a Closed sign up and locked the door, then handed Samantha the check. She and Sean were still holding hands.

I was refilling the syrup containers when there was a knock on the door.

I went to explain to whoever it was that we were closed, but then saw it was Natalie, Slim's girlfriend. Natalie was a witch—a real one.

She had been at a coven training course in Salem for the last few months, and Slim had gone out to visit her a couple of times. Her absence had stymied my efforts to free Lil from the jukebox. Natalie was the only witch I knew, at least the only competent one. Penny Edwards didn't count.

I unlocked the door and let her in. "Welcome home!" I said.

"Hi, Daisy," she said. "I'm glad to be back in Nightshade. Although I learned so much while I was gone."

"Slim will be so glad to see you," I said. "He's been mopey."

Natalie beamed. "I missed him too."

"He's cleaning up in the back," I said. "But do you have a minute? I could use your help."

Natalie wasn't nearly as powerful as Circe Silvertongue, but she was my only hope, especially since Circe had taken her pig and run. Maybe Natalie could at least point me in the right direction.

"I'd be happy to," she said. She shot a longing look toward the kitchen but gave me an encouraging smile just the same.

"You've heard my theory about Lil?"

"That she's really Mrs. Wilder's missing sister Lily? Yes. It seems reasonable."

"And I'm pretty sure that Circe's pet pig, Balthazar, is really Lily Varcol's missing fiancé, Bam Merriweather," I added. "I want to try to break Circe's spell. Can you give me any idea about how to do that? Besides getting Circe to do it herself."

"That's pretty advanced magic," Natalie said. "But if it's the kind of spell I'm thinking of, she might have used objects that were important to the victims to change them."

"She did have this pen she used every day," I said. "It had Bam Merriweather's initials engraved on it."

"Let me look into this," Natalie said. "Most of my grandmother's books are stored in the attic of her house. I'll take a look there, and I might be able to ask some of the more experienced witches."

Natalie's grandmother, Mrs. Mason, had died in a fire that destroyed her greenhouse. She'd been helping the Scourge when she died. She hadn't been a nice person, but she'd been the only relative Natalie had. Fortunately, Natalie had moved in with Slim, and the Mason house stood empty. The gardens, however, were full of gorgeous flowers, fruits, and vegetables, due to the combination of Mrs. Mason's residual magic and Natalie's hard work.

"Thanks, Natalie," I said. "I'd appreciate any help you could give me. Is there anything I can do to help? Research stuff, I mean?"

Natalie thought about it for a second. "Well, you could try the Nightshade City Library," she replied. "Maybe there's a text there that I don't already own."

I agreed to go take a look. I'd comb the dustiest library I could find if it would help.

I could tell by the way Natalie's face lit up that Slim had come out from the kitchen, so I made myself scarce.

"It's closing time," I gently reminded Sam and Sean. As they rose to leave, I overheard a whisper from Sam. "I still think we should tell her."

"Tell me what?" I said sharply.

"Oh, nothing," Sam said. "Just that we're nominating you and Ryan for prom king and queen."

I made a face at her. "Don't you dare," I said. "If anyone should be Nightshade prom queen, it should be you. You were practically born to be queen."

"I have plenty of crowns," she said. "Winning again would be—"

"Awesome," I interrupted her.

"I was going to say overkill," she replied. "C'mon, Daisy. Live a little. It would be fun."

I shrugged. There was no sense in arguing with Sam when she got in this mood.

I shooed them out of the restaurant, then locked up and went home.

To my surprise, all the lights were on at my house when I pulled into the drive. There seemed to be a lot of noise coming from the family room, so I headed that way.

My whole family, including Grandma Giordano, was congregated there.

"What's going on? Why is everyone still up?" I asked.

My father held out a bottle of champagne. "We've been waiting for you," he said. "We're celebrating."

"Celebrating what?" I was completely confused.

"My book deal," Dad said. "I sold my novel."

"What?" I said. "Congratulations! I didn't even know you had finished it."

"It's not finished yet. I still need an ending."

"Why didn't you tell us you were submitting it?" Rose asked.

"I didn't want to say anything at first," Dad said. "I sent it out to a few places, and it got rejected so fast it made my head spin."

"Your father is being modest," Mom said. "It's brilliant."

Grandma Giordano chuckled. "I'm proud of you, son. Now pop that champagne."

A second later, the cork shot out of the bottle and across the room. Poppy went to retrieve it and then handed it to Dad. "You should keep it," she said. "To remember your first sale."

"There's sparkling cider for the girls," Mom said quickly.

"What's the book about?" Poppy said. "Can we read it?"

A shadow passed over Dad's face. "At first I thought I would write a memoir about what happened to me at the hands of the Scourge, but I eventually realized that no one would believe it," he said. "So I did the next best thing. I turned it all into fiction. The Scourge, Nightshade, the kidnapping, everything."

Something about this made me uneasy, but I tried not to show it. I wasn't so sure the Scourge would be happy to be reading about themselves, even in a novel. "What's the title?" I asked.

"Nightshade," he said.

"What?" I said. "Dad!"

"I'm just kidding," he said. "I changed everything, even the names. And it's also based on my research in genetics. It still needs an ending though. I was hoping I would remember something about my kidnapper's identity."

Although Dad didn't remember parts of his abduction, bits and pieces of his captivity were slowly coming back. My parents didn't talk about it much, but Dad was seeing a therapist to help him deal with the trauma of his experience.

"What does Spenser Devereaux think of that?" Grandma asked. "You'll be giving him a run for his money on the bestseller list now."

Dad looked startled. "I told him about the book, but I didn't ask him what he thought of the idea. Spenser took our research and turned it into a bestselling nonfiction book. Mine is fiction. I'm sure he doesn't have a problem with that. We were partners, after all."

"He didn't seem to remember that when he published your findings," Grandma reminded him gently. "He didn't even include your name in the acknowledgments. And everyone knows that you did most of the actual research."

"Spenser has been very supportive," my father insisted. "In fact, he keeps asking to read it, but I told him that I'm keeping certain chapters under wraps until it's published."

Grandma snorted. "Spenser Devereaux is only concerned with Spenser Devereaux."

"Mother, it's fine," he said, but I noticed his hands shook as he poured her a glass of champagne. "No one knew where I was. Spenser needed to forge ahead without me. He already knows I'm writing the book. I will tell him my good news myself."

Mom picked up on Dad's discomfort and changed the subject. "What else did the editor say about your book, dear?"

Talk turned to things like deadlines and covers. I sipped my apple cider and smiled at the sight of my father's face all aglow from his accomplishment. Things would work out for him. They just had to.

CHAPTER TWO

When I got to school the next morning, there was a huge banner in front of the building. It read, VAMPS RULE, WERES DROOL.

A crowd of students had gathered in front of it, and I saw Samantha and some of the other cheerleaders standing there.

"What's that all about?" I asked Sam.

She shrugged. "Boys will be boys," she said. "There have been a few mean-spirited pranks between the shifters and the vampires. Wolfie did something stupid and stirred up the vamps."

"What did he do this time?" I asked.

"No one seems to know," Rachel said.

Jordan nodded. "And Wolfie is staying tightlipped for a change. But the vamps would love to sink their teeth into him."

Wolfgang Paxton was an obnoxious freshman from a Were family. His older brother, Bane, dated Elise Wilder, who was from another prominent Were family. Everyone liked Bane and Elise, but Wolfie was another story.

The whole thing had my classmates on edge. As I walked through the halls, I noticed a lot of snarling and showing of fangs, but nothing physical.

There was one incident, though. Vampires could stand a little bit of sun, but the ones who attended Nightshade came in sunglasses, long coats, and hats. Teachers were usually considerate and kept the window shades drawn.

In English class, Austin Waterman forgot and rolled up one of the shades. As sunlight streamed through the bare window, there was a scream of pain.

"Pull that down, you idiot," I ordered. He did as I told him, but it was too late. McKenna Collins, a vampire girl who normally sat in the back of the class as far from the windows as possible, had been at Mr. Calvado's desk, right in front of the windows. The window shade had been up only for a few minutes, but it let in enough direct sunlight to cause damage to a vampire. Fortunately, she wasn't badly hurt, but she did have to go see Nurse Phillips to have a small burn on her hand treated.

After school, I helped Sam with some yearbook stuff. Everyone on yearbook was talking about the latest incident. Some people even said Austin had done it on purpose. He wasn't a shifter himself, but rumor was that he was dating one.

"He's not that stupid," I protested, but no one listened.

I hoped that the anger between the two groups would blow over in a day or two. Unfortunately, as I left school at dusk I spotted Ryan and Sean squaring off against two angry guys from the football team. It wasn't until I got closer that I realized the two boys were Reese Calhoun and Andres Stewart. Make that two angry vampires.

The object of their dispute was a late-model Chevy with tinted windows, which was covered with some noxious-smelling reddish-brown liquid.

"Pig's blood!" Reese shouted. "Do you know what kind of an insult that is?" He answered his own question. "Of course you do. That's why you did it."

"We didn't do anything," Ryan snarled.

Reese stepped forward until he was standing chest to chest with Ryan. "I don't believe you."

"I don't care what you believe," Ryan replied. "It's the truth."

I stepped between them, ignoring the show of fangs from Reese and the growl from my boyfriend.

"Why don't you both cool off?" I suggested. "Reese, I'd advise you to get to a car wash before that pig blood dries."

"This isn't over," he said, but he and Andres got into the car and departed with a squeal of tires.

Ryan was controlling his temper with difficulty. "Do you think it was a smart idea to step in between a shifter and a vamp?"

"It seemed like a good decision at the time," I said.

"I was handling it," Ryan said.

I raised an eyebrow at his tone. "That's not what it looked

like to me. You and Reese are teammates. Why were you fighting?"

Sean hurried away from us, saying "I, uh, forgot something in my locker."

Ryan took a deep breath and jammed his hands into his pockets. "There's been a little tension between the vampires and the shifters lately."

"But Reese knows you. He knows you'd never do anything like that," I said.

"Lines are being drawn, Daisy," he said wearily. "If something doesn't change soon, everyone in Nightshade will have to choose a side."

"Can't the council do anything?" I asked.

"They're trying," he said. "But ever since that Were football player in San Carlos was killed, it's been tense between the vampires and shifters."

"That happened back in October," I said. I was certain he wasn't telling me everything.

"Since then, there have been a few incidents," he replied.

"Incidents?" I repeated.

"Yeah, incidents."

"Care to elaborate?"

"It's Were business, Daisy," he told me.

I knew the confrontation with Reese had him on edge, but I was irritated too.

As Ryan drove me home, I couldn't stop thinking about

what had happened. I didn't want to believe that the citizens of Nightshade could be involved in hating each other just because of their differences, but I wasn't so naive that I didn't know that people hated each other for a variety of stupid reasons.

I said a quick good night to Ryan and then headed inside. I wanted to talk to my sisters about the fighting between the two paranormal factions.

Turns out they were already discussing it. Loudly.

"You don't know what you're talking about," Poppy yelled. "There's no way the vampires started this mess."

Rose was outwardly calmer than Poppy, but I could tell she was on the brink of completely losing it.

What's going on? I sent her the message covertly, but Poppy caught me. "It figures you'd take her side," she said. "You both date shifters. You're ganging up on me because I'm dating a vampire."

"Ganging up?" I said aloud. "I just got home. Besides, we didn't even know Liam *was* a vampire. The only time I saw him was at the ball for about ten seconds."

"I can't believe my own family is so prejudiced," Poppy said. She actually stomped her feet. Logic didn't work with Poppy when she was all riled up, and she was on a complete tear.

"Isn't dating a vampire a little dangerous?" I asked.

"You mean, because he's a deadly paranormal creature who can't always control himself?" she said. "Like, oh, I don't know, a *werewolf*?"

"It's not the same thing," I protested. "Ryan would never hurt me."

"And Liam would never hurt me," Poppy replied.

Fortunately, Mom walked in and put a stop to the argument.

"What's going on?" she asked. "I could hear you fighting all the way outside."

"Poppy thinks that we're ganging up on her because she's dating a vampire," Rose said. "It's not our fault she's too embarrassed to bring him home."

"I'm not embarrassed of *him*," Poppy said.

Rose stuck out her tongue at her.

"Poppy, I think it's time we got to know your young man," Mom said. "Maybe a family dinner will put a stop to all this Team Fangs or Team Fur nonsense."

She didn't seem all that surprised to hear Poppy was dating a vampire. Maybe it was only Rose and me that Poppy had been shutting out.

"Dad will grill him mercilessly," Poppy protested.

"Probably," Mom replied. "But Liam is coming to dinner anyway."

A tiny bit of me felt sorry for Poppy, but only a minuscule portion. She'd thought it was hilarious when Dad had given Ryan the third degree.

"Not so funny now, is it?" I couldn't resist poking at her.

"Invite Ryan and the chief too," Mom said. "Rose, I expect to see Nicholas and his dad at our little dinner party as well."

There was no arguing with Mom when she took that tone.

Rose and Poppy stomped off in different directions and I stared after them, perplexed. They'd always been close—so close that sometimes I'd felt completely left out—and I wasn't used to seeing my two sisters screaming at each other. The animosity between shifters and vampires was the real root of the problem. But Dad's perfect soufflé wasn't going to solve the issue. Not for my sisters, and definitely not for Nightshade.

CHAPTER THREE

The doorbell rang promptly at six thirty the next evening. Ryan was early, but fortunately I was ready. I'd borrowed a bright pink dress from my more fashion-forward sister Poppy. I rarely wore lighter colors, since I found it was hard to get bloodstains out of those shades, but the color suited me. More important, I was fairly certain that nothing involving murder or mayhem would happen tonight. At least, I hoped not.

I answered the door. Ryan looked gorgeous in crisply pressed trousers and a dark green sweater that matched his eyes. My palms were sweating. Even after over a year together, the sight of him made my heart accelerate. He was gorgeous, but it was his smile that really got me.

"Hi, Daisy," he said. "Ready to go?"

"Let me get my jacket," I said. Since it was only March, the evenings were still cool in Northern California.

I started to put it on, but Ryan was there before me. Those quick Were reflexes of his.

"I'll get it," he said. He held out my jacket. He smelled great, like fresh clean skin with just a hint of soap and anxiety.

I tried to put my arms into the sleeves, but Ryan fumbled with the jacket, nearly losing his grip. If I didn't know better, I'd say he was nervous.

I gave him an inquiring look, but he just smiled sheepishly.

When we arrived at Wilder's Restaurant, Bianca was acting as hostess and seating people. Like the Wilder family, Bianca was a shifter. She was also my own personal guardian angel. Or more accurately, my own guardian kitten, because that's what she shifted into—a black kitten. She'd saved my butt on more than one occasion.

"It's so nice to see you," she said. "Any news about colleges yet?"

"Not yet," I replied. "Ryan hasn't heard anything either. The suspense is killing us."

Ryan shifted on his feet and looked at the floor. He was definitely acting weird tonight.

"I'm sure you'll hear soon," Bianca replied. "Now let me show you to your table. I think you'll be pleased."

She led us into one of the smaller rooms just off the main dining room. We were the only two people in the room, and a cozy fire crackled in the fireplace.

"Your server will be with you shortly," she said, and turned to leave the room.

"Bianca, wait—there's one other thing," I said, remembering my promise to Lil.

She paused. "Yes?"

"Can I come by and talk to you soon? I have some questions for you about Circe Silvertongue."

"Of course," she said. "Anytime."

"Great," I said. I turned my attention back to my date.

There was an awkward silence after Bianca excused herself. Ryan stared resolutely at his menu.

"You wanted to talk to me about something?" I prompted him.

"It can wait," he said. "Let's order first. What are you going to have?"

We sat there talking about food, like two strangers. Whatever Ryan had to tell me, I was pretty sure I wasn't going to like it.

And I was right.

He waited until after we had enjoyed our meal. Although *enjoyed* might not be the best description. The lump in my throat made it hard to swallow, which meant I was only picking at my food, and I noticed that Ryan barely touched his steak tartare, which was a specialty at Wilder's.

I knew Ryan wasn't going to break up with me—at least, I was pretty sure. My mind reeled with horrible possibilities, so at first I was relieved when he cleared his throat and said, "I wanted to talk to you about college."

That's all? Giddy with relief, I beamed at him.

"That's the first smile I've seen all night," he said. He smiled back at me, but he still looked nervous.

I was suddenly starving, so I dove into my creamy mashed potatoes and baked chicken.

"I signed a letter of intent a couple of weeks ago," he blurted out.

My fork, which had been halfway to my mouth, clattered to the floor. "You what?"

"I'm playing baseball for UC Irvine," he said.

UCI was in Orange County, hundreds of miles away.

I was speechless. My face felt hot, and I reached for my glass of water, hoping to cool down.

"I wanted to tell you," he continued.

"But you didn't," I said. I could hear my voice getting louder, but I couldn't help myself. I was hurt. My mind flashed to Sam and Sean. She was staying here and he was leaving, but she'd known right away. Sean had been completely honest with Sam. Ryan had not done the same with me. And I didn't know why. Our solid foundation suddenly seemed shaky.

"Daisy," Ryan said. "Don't be mad."

Mad was an understatement. I was furious.

"Is that why you brought me here?" I said. "You think a fancy dinner is going to make up for lying to me for weeks?"

"Daisy, I'm sorry," he said, twisting his napkin in his hands until it shredded.

"What about staying here? What about staying in Nightshade with me?"

"I don't want to leave you," he said. "But I don't want to stay in Nightshade my whole life either."

That stopped me in midharangue.

"You don't? But we talked about it."

"No, *you* talked about it," he replied. "It's different for me. Don't you think I can make it in the outside world?"

"Of course you can," I said. "But what about during the full moon?"

"Elise is away at college. Bane too," he argued. Elise Wilder and Bane Paxton were both shape-shifters, werewolves to be exact.

I shook my head. "No, they *tried* it. Elise's been back for weeks, and Bane's due home any day."

"Something you neglected to tell me," he said sharply.

I glared at him. I couldn't help it. I felt abandoned.

"You're the one who knows all about 'Were business,' so I figured you would know," I snapped.

"Daisy, sometimes it's best to leave paranormal issues up to the city council," Ryan said. "Do you really expect me to tell you everything that goes on in the Were community? Should I tell you what I had for breakfast too?"

"Don't bother," I said. I threw my napkin onto the table and stormed off.

I knew he'd stop to pay the bill but he still caught up with me halfway to the car. Weres could move fast when they wanted.

"Don't be silly," he said. "I'll drive you home."

And that was the last thing he said to me for the rest of the night.

CHAPTER FOUR

It was Friday, a week later, but we had a day off from school. Some sort of special teacher training day.

Since we had a free day, Samantha and I were hanging out in my room. She had a UC Nightshade brochure and was showing me the dorm photos. "Aren't they cool?"

"You're not going to be living at home?" I asked. Her dad's condo was walking distance from the campus.

I shoved aside the envy I was feeling. It wasn't Sam's fault that I hadn't heard anything from Nightshade, or from any other school for that matter.

She shrugged. "Dad already put down a deposit on a single. He said he's going to be traveling a lot next year for his book tour. Besides, he thinks I should live in the dorms to get the full college experience."

"I guess Ryan will be living in a dorm," I said. "Not that he's told me anything."

"Are you two still fighting?" she asked sympathetically.

I nodded. I hadn't talked to Ryan since I'd stormed out of

the restaurant, except in class, and that didn't count. He'd managed to find somewhere else to be at lunch all week. He was avoiding me.

"Ryan's never been mad at me before. Not really. Not like this," I told her.

"Don't take this the wrong way, Daisy, but I don't really blame him," she said.

"Hey, I thought you were *my* best friend," I said.

"I am," she assured me. "And that's why I'm being completely honest with you. You were kind of, well, oblivious to his feelings. Sean said he wanted to share his big news with you sooner, but he knew you wouldn't be happy about it because you want him to stay in Nightshade."

I considered what Sam said for a moment. She was right.

"You need to do something, and soon," she continued. "These little fights can snowball into something permanent unless somebody makes the first move. And in this case, it should be you."

"I know," I said. "Even though Ryan didn't tell me he'd already signed with a college, I was the one who lost my temper. I owe him an apology."

Sam gave me an encouraging thumbs-up.

I took a deep breath and picked up the phone.

"Hello?" The sound of his voice flooded me with relief. He wasn't so mad that he ignored my call.

"I'm a terrible girlfriend," I said. "That is, if I still *am* your girlfriend."

"Of course you're still my girlfriend," he said. "It's just, you don't understand how it is for me."

"I'll try," I promised. "Let me make it up to you," I added. "Are you free tomorrow night? I'll cook you dinner."

"You don't have to," he said.

"No, I want to," I replied. "I was completely insensitive. I'll make chicken mole. Your favorite." Ryan loved it, but authentic mole sauce was tricky to make and took a long time.

After I hung up with Ryan, I gave Sam a hug.

"What was that for?" she asked, but there was a smile on her face.

"Thanks for the advice," I said. "Want to go to the grocery store with me?"

"No thanks," she said, barely repressing a shudder. "I'm heading over to Sean's. He just sent me a text that he misses me."

"How are you guys going to handle the whole distance thing?" I asked.

She shrugged. "We'll make it work," she said. "It's only for a few months at a time. If you love someone, you should be willing to wait."

After Sam left, I went into the kitchen to check supplies. I wanted to make fresh tortillas and beans to serve with the chicken mole. The cupboards were bare. Well, not bare exactly, but I would definitely need to make a trip to the store to get all the ingredients. And I needed to make some sort of delicious dessert for a fabulous finale to my "I screwed up" dinner menu.

I went to the foot of the stairs. "Mom, can I borrow your car?" I called up to her. "I need to go to the grocery store. I'm making dinner for Ryan tomorrow night."

I heard her footsteps, and then she appeared.

"Of course," she said. "Would you mind picking up a few other things if I give you a list? I've been swamped at work."

"Sure, I can pick up anything you need," I said.

"Just be careful out there," she said. "There are some strange things happening in Nightshade."

Stranger than usual? I sent her an inquiring look, but she didn't elaborate.

I scooped up the car keys and headed to the store.

An hour later, it was just past dusk and I was walking to my car, loaded down with groceries, when I heard a strange choking sound coming from the bushes to my left.

There was a trail of blood glistening on the sidewalk, and it looked fresh. I set the bags down with a thump.

I ignored my fear and pulled out my cell phone. I punched in the emergency number and then said, "This is Daisy Giordano. I'm in the parking lot of Galaxy Groceries, and there's blood all over the sidewalk. Could you send someone out?"

I heard another moan, but my psychic abilities didn't pick

up anything. Someone was clearly in pain. I couldn't just stand there, so I followed the blood. My heart raced as I clutched my cell phone in my hand. I'd been in danger before, but I knew someone needed my help and I had a feeling it couldn't wait.

Still, I felt sick when I saw the body lying face down. Blood pooled and then spread in tiny rivulets. The figure was female, and something told me she was around my age. The blood seemed to be coming from her neck.

I took off my scarf and applied pressure to the wound. The young woman's hair was matted with blood, and the smell overwhelmed me. I fought retching. I hoped help would be there soon. It seemed like an hour had passed, but I realized it had only been a few minutes.

"Daisy?" came her faint voice.

Dread filled me. It was someone I knew. Or, at least, someone who knew me.

"Turn me over, please." I was so upset, I couldn't tell if the conversation was happening in my mind or if she'd spoken aloud.

I did as she asked and flipped her over, as gently as I could, but she smothered a scream of pain. When I saw her, I wanted to throw up.

A huge piece of her throat had been torn out. Somehow, though, she was saying something. I recognized the voice. "Elise? Elise Wilder?"

"It's me," she said. "There's not much time."

Her voice was fading, and I bent closer. She said something I couldn't hear.

"It's okay, don't talk," I told her.

Not. Talking, she sent back.

This time I knew I was reading her mind. She sent me another message, but it was blurred by her pain. Then, more clearly, *Vamps.*

"You mean vampires did this to you?" I asked, but the connection was gone. She'd lost consciousness.

I was relieved to hear the ambulance. I waited until I heard the sound of someone approaching. "We're over here. Please hurry! She's hurt badly."

Two emergency response people took charge. I stood there feeling helpless as they loaded Elise into the ambulance and took off, headed for the hospital.

Ryan and his dad came roaring up in his dad's police car. Ryan jumped out and came running toward me.

"What happened? Are you okay?"

I seemed to have a knack for finding bodies, dead or otherwise.

I inhaled shakily. "I'm fine. Ryan, it was Elise Wilder. It looked like someone had slashed her throat. There was blood everywhere."

He wrapped his arms around me.

Chief Mendez joined us. "Daisy, are you up to answering

a few questions right now? I'd like to get the information while it's still fresh."

I nodded and then filled him in on how I found her.

"Did she say anything?" Chief Mendez asked.

I hesitated. "I'm not sure I heard correctly."

"Just tell me what you think you heard," he replied.

"'Vamps,'" I said. "She said 'vamps.'"

I'd never seen that expression on the chief's face before, but I wasn't imagining the emotion I saw. He looked scared.

CHAPTER FIVE

After I had answered the chief's questions, Ryan helped me gather up the groceries and put them in the trunk of my car.

He drove me home in my car because my hands were shaking too much for me to drive.

When we got home, my sisters came running to meet us.

"Mom is freaking out," Rose warned me.

"She heard something happened at the grocery store," Poppy said.

"Something did," I said. My mind flashed to the horrible scene. Elise lying on the ground, her throat a jagged slash of red.

Ryan wrapped his arm around me. "Let's go inside," he said. "Daisy can tell you all about it in a bit. She's a little shaken up."

Once inside, we ran into my mom in the hallway. She had car keys in hand and was clearly on her way out. "Daisy, Chief Mendez called me and told me what happened. I'm on my way to the crime scene right now."

She paused for a moment and gave me a long hug. "I've got to go, but we'll talk later, honey. Your sisters are here, and if you need anything, call my cell."

"Be careful, Mom," I said.

"You too," she said. "Don't answer the door unless you know who it is, and even then be cautious."

I nodded, and then we went into the kitchen.

"I'll make you some tea," Rose said.

"You're lucky Dad's still at the library," Poppy commented. "You know he'd freak out."

Rose shot her a dirty look. "You're not helping, Poppy."

She stuck her tongue out at Rose. "I'll find some cookies," Poppy said to me. "Sugar's good for you. You've had a shock."

"Isn't that for when you give blood?" Ryan asked.

The word *blood* reminded me of Elise and how much of her blood had been all over.

I sat down hard on a kitchen stool.

"Sorry," Ryan said. "I spoke before I thought."

"It's okay," I said.

Rose put a steaming cup of mint tea in front of me and spooned a liberal helping of honey into it. "Drink this," she ordered. "I'll take care of the groceries."

Poppy handed me a cookie. I was lucky to have sisters who cared so much about me.

I took a sip of the tea, then took a deep breath and told them the whole story.

Before I could finish, Dad came rushing in, followed closely by Rose's boyfriend, Nicholas.

"Daisy! Thank goodness you're not hurt," Dad said.

I was happy to see he wasn't shaking. He'd been abducted by the Scourge when I was little and had only recently come back home. Overprotective was an understatement.

I started from the beginning again and then finished with what I'd heard Elise say. "Vamps."

"And you're sure that's what you heard?" Nicholas asked. He was pretty intense about it, but I knew he'd tell his dad, who was the head of the Nightshade City Council.

"I'm sure," I said. I'd gone over it in my mind about a million times since I found her.

Poppy crossed her arms over her chest. "You must have heard wrong, Daisy," she said flatly.

What's her problem? I sent a message to Rose telepathically, but Poppy caught on.

"Stop that, you two," she said. "If you have something to say, then say it."

"Okay," I said. "Why are you acting so weird about this? You're acting like I accused *you* of attacking Elise."

"I just think you may be jumping to conclusions is all," she said.

I shrugged. "Maybe, but I heard what I heard. The chief said he'll look into it. So, you can't tell anyone what I told you."

"I'll let the council know," Nicholas said.

"My dad said he'd give your dad a call," Ryan said. Chief Mendez and Mr. Bone worked together to keep Nightshade safe.

Poppy still looked irate, but there was nothing I could do to appease her when she was in this mood.

"I want you girls to be careful," Dad said.

"We will," Rose soothed him.

Dad changed the subject. "Who's hungry? I'll order takeout."

The thought of food made me want to gag, but I didn't want to disappoint Dad. He always wanted to feed everyone when there was a crisis.

"How does apology Thai food sound?" I asked Ryan.

"Not as good as your chicken mole, but you know me, I'm always hungry," he replied. He gave it his best effort, but his smile didn't reach his eyes.

"She'll be okay," I said softly. I wasn't sure if I was telling the truth, but I prayed Elise would pull through. Elise had helped Ryan through a difficult time, when he first learned to deal with shifting. She had really been there when Ryan needed someone who understood what being a shifter meant. Nicholas had tried to help Ryan, but two male Weres in the same room didn't necessarily equal peace and tranquility. He and Ryan got along fine now, though, which was a relief.

"We'll find out who did this to her," I added.

This time, his smile was a real one. "Daisy Giordano is on the case," he said.

I glanced over at Dad, but he hadn't heard us, thankfully. He and Nicholas were talking about Dad's new book deal.

I wondered what the council would think of Dad writing about Nightshade secrets, but I got my answer seconds later.

"Your father suggested that I use a pen name," Dad said to Nicholas. "And the town is now in Oregon instead of California."

"I can't wait to read it," Nicholas responded.

Mom came back just as we sat down to dine on Thai One On's signature dish, the spicy Crying Tiger.

Dad got up from the table. "Sit down, honey, and let me fix you a plate."

"It smells delicious," Mom said. She plopped down on a seat next to Dad's and kicked off her shoes.

"How did it go?" Poppy asked.

"You know I don't want you guys involved in this," she said.

"Mom, Elise is our friend. I found her near death. We're already involved," I said.

Mom sighed. "You're right," she said. "It was exactly like that other vampire case. I couldn't pick up a trace. Not a single clue. I couldn't even sense my own daughter's presence at the scene. I was useless."

Mom's specialty was psychometry, which she used to help the police at crime scenes. Like, if someone died, she could sometimes figure out how by touching something that belonged to the person or an object from the crime scene.

"Maybe good old-fashioned forensics will turn up something," Dad said.

"Or Elise will regain consciousness," I said.

"They induced a coma," Mom said. "Poor girl was in too much pain. And . . ."

"She tried to shift, didn't she?" Nicholas said.

Mom nodded. "She's in her human form, and I hope she's dreaming peacefully. Mrs. Wilder hired a private nurse, so that helps."

"Why would a vampire attack Elise?" Ryan said.

"In a word, food," Nicholas replied.

"Gross," Poppy said. "Besides that weird soul-sucking vamp from last year, there haven't been any vampire attacks in ages."

"This was definitely an old-fashioned bloodsucker," I said. "Her throat looked like hamburger meat." I pushed away my food. I'd lost what little appetite I'd had. "But if it wasn't a vampire, what was it? Who or what could do that to Elise?"

No one had an answer, but I wasn't really expecting one.

CHAPTER SIX

The next day I was scheduled for an early shift at Slim's. The morning fog made Nightshade's familiar Main Street look foreign and vaguely menacing. I was glad that Mom was dropping me off on her way to work.

Flo was already there when I arrived. She wore a T-shirt that read I'M A GLEEK. A sign of a kinder, gentler Flo?

She caught me staring at her shirt and actually blushed a little. "It's a gift from Vinnie," she said. Vinnie was her boyfriend and was in my favorite band, Side Effects May Vary, along with Nightshade High's school nurse, Ms. Phillips.

"Did he mean it ironically?" I asked, having a hard time picturing it.

She giggled. "No, he's a total fan," she said.

"He has good taste," I said. "In girlfriends and in television shows."

It wasn't until a little before lunch that things went downhill. Wolfgang Paxton walked in the door with some of his buddies. I sighed and gave Flo an imploring look, which she ignored. I was stuck waiting on them. No sense in putting off the inevitable, so I grabbed some menus and headed over to their table.

"What can I get you?"

"Hi, Daisy," Wolfgang said with a wink. "I'm glad you asked."

What horrible innuendo would come out of his mouth? Wolfie was an all-around pain in the butt, but he was also a paying customer.

I gave him a tightlipped smile. "What do you want for *lunch?*" I asked emphatically.

He had the grace to apologize. "Sorry, I can see you're busy. Can we get three rare cheeseburgers, two large fries, and three chocolate shakes?"

"And a steak platter," one of his buddies said. "The twenty-four ounce."

"Rare, I take it?"

Wolfgang nodded. "And when you have time, I need to talk to you about something." He read the reluctance on my face. "It's important."

"Okay," I agreed, "but it'll have to wait until my break."

I had fully expected him to eat and run—after paying the check, of course—but when I finally caught my breath, Wolfgang was still sitting at the table, alone, patiently waiting.

The diner had almost emptied out, and Flo had already plopped down on her favorite stool at the counter. I made myself an iced coffee and offered money to Flo, which she waved away.

"Is it okay if I take my break now?" I asked her.

"Fine with me," she said.

I went to talk to Wolfgang, who was gnawing on a few remaining fries on his plate.

"What do you want, Wolfie?" I asked. I was being kind of rude, I knew, but he was kind of a jerk.

"It's not anything bad," he replied. "I wanted to say thank you for helping Elise."

I couldn't have been more floored if he'd wanted to elope.

After I recovered from my surprise, I asked, "How is she? I'd like to stop by and see her after my shift."

"She's still not conscious," he said grimly. "Bane won't leave her bedside, not even to sleep, but he wanted me to tell you he's very grateful. They said she might not have made it if you hadn't come along when you did."

I didn't know what to say. Whoever had done that to Elise was a truly evil person, but after a lot of thought, I wasn't sure that it really was a vampire. First of all, what vampire was foolhardy enough to take on the entire Wilder clan? Not to mention the Paxtons, who were another very powerful Were family. Plus, it was barely past dusk when I found her, and vampires don't like daylight. But I was positive Elise had communicated the word *vamp* to me. What else could she have meant?

Wolfgang's lower lip quivered, but with effort he controlled his emotions. "I want you to tell me everything you know about what happened."

"I heard moaning and saw the blood. I went to help her. You know the rest."

"Did she say anything when you found her?" he persisted.

"She was in a lot of pain," I replied.

"Please, Daisy," he said. "Bane's going crazy, wondering why anyone would do that to Elise."

I hesitated. "Chief Mendez asked me not to discuss the particulars of the case." And to stay out of the investigation, but I had no intention of doing that.

"It was a vampire. That's what everyone's saying," Wolfgang said. The anger in his voice was so intense that I shivered. He was out for payback.

"Maybe there's another explanation," I said. I was already breaking my promise not to talk.

"Please, Daisy," he said in a gentler tone. "We want to know who's behind this, and we know the city council isn't exactly impartial when it comes to crimes committed by paranormals. You've got to help us." The distress on Wolfie's face convinced me.

"I'll look into it," I said. "But I'm not making any promises."

He nodded. "That's good enough for me."

He got up to leave, but I thought of something else. "Do you know of any reason a vampire would be angry at Elise? Or Bane?"

"No clue," he replied, but he said it to his shoes. I did a little mental probe and caught the words *my fault* before he left. Wolfie was guilt ridden about something. He irritated everyone—maybe this time he'd ticked off the wrong person and Elise had paid the price.

When I got home from work, there was a pink '57 T-bird in our driveway. It was a dead ringer for Miss Foster's car, but my former gym teacher wouldn't be driving anymore. I'd turned her into an oily splotch on the gymnasium floor, hadn't I?

"What's that thing doing in our driveway?" I demanded as soon as I got into the house.

"Isn't she great?" Dad replied. "I've always wanted one, you know. I bought it with some of my book advance."

I wanted to be happy for him, but my stomach lurched at the thought of seeing it every day. "Where did you find it?"

"Spenser gave me the lead," he said. "It used to belong to an old friend of his."

My unease grew. "Who?"

"Spenser," Dad said. "Spenser Devereaux, Samantha's dad, my colleague." His twinkling eyes gave away that he was teasing.

"That's not what I mean, Dad," I said. "I mean, who did the car belong to?"

He shrugged. "Spenser didn't say. He told me that his friend wouldn't be needing it any longer."

My stomach clenched, but I told myself that it was probably just a coincidence. Then again, exactly how many pink T-birds were there in Nightshade?

CHAPTER SEVEN

Things seemed to calm down in Nightshade after Elise's attack. At least, I thought so until about a week later, when Sam came up to me after my last class. "Have you heard what they're saying?"

"What?"

"That there's going to be a fight in Nightshade. The vamps against the Weres."

"Where did you hear that?"

"Penny told me," she said. "Tyler overheard some of the guys talking about it."

You could count on Penny to know the latest gossip, although she'd tapered off a bit since she and Tyler had gotten serious.

"What has everyone in an uproar this time?" I asked.

"Didn't you know?" Sam asked. "There was another one. Two nights ago. They're trying to keep it quiet. Christy Hannigan's mom works at the hospital, and she told Christy all about it."

"Another Were was attacked?"

Sam shook her head somberly. "No, it was a vampire this time. One of the young ones. And now the vampires are out for blood. Literally."

"That can't be good," I said. I couldn't believe I was so behind on the gossip, but then again, we didn't know all the vamps in town since some of them went to night school.

We walked to the car.

"Hey, do you want to spend the night at my house?" Sam asked. "My dad's out of town and it's a little spooky there by myself."

"I thought you'd want to spend every waking moment with Sean," I said.

"Oh, he and his dad are going on that father-son camping trip with Ryan and the chief."

"I could use a break from my sisters."

"I don't blame you," she said. "It must be tough."

"I was just kidding," I said. "What must be tough?"

"Forget I said anything," Sam replied.

"Come on, Sam," I said.

"It's just, I thought Rose and Poppy might be having some problems," she said. "Since Rose is dating a shifter and Poppy is dating a vampire."

"They're getting along fine," I said. I was totally in denial. They still weren't getting along at all. Hopefully, Mom's dinner party would solve that problem.

"Of course they are," she said soothingly.

She looked so abashed that I couldn't say no to her invitation. "Let me just clear it with my parents," I said.

We stopped at my house for a change of clothes and my sleeping bag before heading to Sam's. I'd been to Mr. Devereaux's condo a few times, but it had been mostly right after Sam had moved in with him. The place had changed since my last visit.

"Your father redecorated," I said.

The condo, which had been nice before, was now opulent. The modest television had been replaced by a gargantuan flatscreen TV that took up one entire wall. When I stepped on the white carpet it felt like I was walking on down pillows, and there was a white silk couch against the other wall that looked too pristine too sit on.

"Let's put your stuff in my room," Sam suggested. As we walked down the hall, I noticed that snapshots of Sam had been replaced by several paintings. I stopped for a second and examined one with multicolored splatters.

"This looks like a real Jackson Pollock," I said.

Sam shrugged. "One of Dad's former students painted it. He said she gave him a good deal."

Mr. Devereaux seemed to have a lot of cash lately. *His book must be doing well,* I thought.

We stashed my stuff in her room, which looked like it was

the only part of the place that hadn't had a makeover, and then headed back to the living room.

"Do you want to go rent a movie or something?" I said.

"We have plenty of movies here," Sam said. She opened a cabinet full of DVDs. "Dad just bought the newest Matt Damon film," she said.

"Didn't that just come out?"

She shrugged. "He buys a lot of movies," she said. "But he never seems to have time to watch them."

She saw my sympathetic smile and said, "Don't feel sorry for me, Daisy. My dad's busy, but he loves me."

"What's not to love?" I replied.

She bumped my shoulder. "Now, let's pick out a movie. What do you want? Action adventure? Horror? Romantic comedy?"

"I've had enough horror in my life lately," I answered. "So no vampires fighting with werewolves. How about a nice, safe romantic comedy?"

"Want some popcorn?" Samantha said.

"Can we eat in here?"

"Sure," she said. "Dad said everything can be replaced."

Her dad seemed fairly cool about his new possessions, especially considering that the Devereaux family had been having financial problems not that long ago.

"How about I make some caramel corn?" I said. My

stomach growled. The fries we'd split at Slim's obviously hadn't satisfied my hunger pangs.

"And let's get a pizza," she replied. "Dad left me a bunch of cash." She took out a stack of what looked like hundreds and took out a bill, then replaced the money in the kitchen drawer.

After we ordered a large pizza with chicken, white sauce, and extra garlic, I started on the caramel corn. I popped the kernels and then put a stick of butter into a shiny new high-end copper pot and turned the burner on low heat.

The doorbell rang, and I assumed it was the pizza delivery person, but then I heard Samantha and it sounded like she was arguing with someone. Something in her voice made me shut off the stove and rush to the front door.

"No, he's not here right now," she said. "Can I take a message?"

"What's up?" I said, moving in front of her protectively.

"She's here for my father," Sam said. "Who, as I said before," she emphasized, "Is. Not. Here."

The woman's face was in shadow, but she gave an annoyed grunt at the news that Mr. Devereaux was not available. A hat concealed most of her face, but I noticed a small purplish birthmark on her jaw.

"I'll wait," she said, and made an attempt to push her way in. I slammed the door in her face and threw the deadbolt.

"I must see him," she said. "It's important or I wouldn't be here. Tell him it's Trinity."

"Go away," I shouted through the door. "Right now, or I'm calling the cops."

Sam had already grabbed the phone, but the stranger gave up. Her heels clicked as she walked away.

"Do you think we should call the police?" she asked.

"No, she was probably just . . ." I hesitated, not sure of a polite way to put it.

"Looking for a booty call?" Sam collapsed into a fit of giggles. "Gross, Giordano."

"I just meant, you know, after the divorce, your dad probably wants to, er, date again."

"I can't say much for his choice of women," she said. "First Ms. Tray, and now this weirdo."

Ms. Tray had been our high school guidance counselor for a very short time. She was attractive on the outside but pure evil on the inside.

"I've heard it's tough to be single," I said. I smothered a few giggles of my own. "I think I recognized her, though."

"I've never seen her before," Sam said.

"I think she's the substitute postal carrier," I said. "She was delivering mail on my street the other day."

"Whoever she is, she's weird," Sam said. "I hope Dad isn't serious about her."

When the doorbell rang again a few minutes later, we both jumped, but it was only the pizza guy.

"Thanks for staying with me, Daisy," Samantha said. "You're a good friend."

I was embarrassed by her gratitude. "You have caramel corn in your teeth," I said.

She laughed. "Cut it out," she said. "And just take my thank-you."

"Okay," I said. "You're welcome. Now hand over a slice of that pizza." And I took a huge bite so I wouldn't start blubbering. This might be one of the last nights like this, especially if I didn't get into UC Nightshade.

Sam read my mind. "You'll get in, Daisy. I know it."

The rest of the night was filled with calories, gossip, and fun. Thankfully, the strange woman did not make another appearance.

CHAPTER EIGHT

After work on Saturday, I decided to head out to do some research. So much had happened that my promise to Lil had nearly slipped my mind. My first stop was the library, where I combed every shelf and searched for the type of books Natalie had suggested. I was dusty and hot when I ran into my favorite librarian, Ms. Johns. Her curly brown hair was longer than when I'd seen her last, but her merry smile was the same as I remembered.

"Daisy, I haven't seen you for ages!" she said.

"I know," I said. "I've been so busy lately."

"We just got some wonderful new cookbooks in," she said.

"Thanks, but I'm looking for something a little bit different today," I replied.

"What exactly are you looking for?" she asked.

I lowered my voice. "Do you have any specialty stacks?"

She frowned in puzzlement. "I don't know what you mean."

"Stuff only certain people in Nightshade would want to read?"

"You're going to have to narrow it down a bit," she said.

"I'm looking for a way to break a spell," I finally blurted out. I knew I could trust her. She was a librarian, after all. It was their job to save lives with books.

She didn't even pretend to look surprised but tapped a finger on her chin while she thought. "I've got it!" She snapped her fingers. "It's in a private collection."

She led me to a tiny room near the children's storytime tent. A metal desk was against one wall, and books were stacked in every available space. She ignored the shelves to focus on the books in a locked display case.

"I thought so," she said. She produced a tiny key and twisted it in the lock.

She thumbed through a couple of texts, then settled on a large leather-bound book. She handed it to me carefully. It felt like it weighed about fifty pounds.

"They used to cover books in human skin," she said. I nearly dropped the book I was holding.

She laughed. "Oh, not this one."

"Why was it locked up?" I asked.

"This is part of my private collection," she said. "I know you'll take good care of it."

She checked her watch. "I'll be back in about an hour

to check in on you," she said. "I hope you find what you're look-ing for."

I hoped so, too. I sat on the floor and started reading, turn-ing the pages gingerly. About halfway through the large tome, I spotted something promising. I marked the page with a piece of scrap paper.

Ms. Johns poked her head in the doorway. "Did you find anything helpful?"

"I think I did," I said. "Can I borrow this one too?" I pointed to another book. The title was *Witchcraft for Dummies*, which seemed like something I could read quickly.

"Certainly," she said.

"And now, where are those cookbooks you mentioned?" There were some thank-you brownies in Ms. Johns's future.

I was reading the books I'd checked out from the library when Rose knocked on my door. I was relieved to see her, because my thoughts kept turning back to the latest attack instead of staying on the words in front of me.

"Council meeting tonight," she said.

"Should we go?" I asked, but I already knew the answer. There was a mystery to solve, which meant it was time to attend another Nightshade City Council meeting.

It wasn't exactly that we weren't welcome at the meetings, but my sisters and I usually tried to keep a low profile, which is why we tried to sneak in after the meeting had already started. We were minus Poppy, which was unusual. When we'd told her about the meeting, she'd murmured something vague about meeting us there.

Rose was behind the wheel. "Did Nicholas say where tonight's meeting is?" I asked her.

"His dad's funeral parlor," she said. Her boyfriend, Nicholas, usually filled us in on council events.

We hadn't mentioned our destination to our parents, but we did tell them we'd be home late. Otherwise, Dad would have had Chief Mendez searching for us. I blushed as I recalled the particularly embarrassing time when the chief found Ryan and me making out in the front seat of Ryan's car. Not my finest moment.

When we arrived at Mort's Mortuary, the parking lot was full and there were cars parked down the street and around the block too.

"That's weird," Rose said. "Why are so many people here tonight?"

We finally found a parking spot three blocks away and walked to the mortuary. When we got there, Nicholas came rushing down the hall toward us. "Thank god you're here," he said. "Things are out of control."

"What's wrong?" I asked.

"It's shifters versus vampires in there," he replied. "And if Dad doesn't get here soon, there's going to be a brawl."

"Where is he?" Rose asked.

"He's supposed to be here already," Nicholas replied. He ran his hand through his red hair.

Someone started pounding on the front door. Nicholas flinched, then turned to Rose. "I'll be right back."

Should we go in? I sent the thought to Rose, but she only shook her head in response. I couldn't resist opening the door and peeking in. I heard her thoughts very clearly: *Oh my god.*

Our sister Poppy was sitting smack in the middle of a den of hungry-looking vampires. There was a distinguished-looking man in an expensive suit who leaned on a long silver cane as he paced. He wasn't anyone I'd ever seen before, but he was handsome.

"This will not stand," he said. He had a voice like Vincent Price, full of menace. The sound was guaranteed to send shivers down a listener's spine.

Poppy saw us and waved. "It's about time you got here. What are you doing standing in the doorway? Come in already."

I noticed that she was holding hands with Liam. My sister had had her heart broken not that long ago, so normally I'd be happy to see her date anyone—vampire, Were, or swamp monster—if it made her happy. I had nothing against vampires, at least in theory, but with the escalating tensions between the Weres and the vampires, I had a feeling that the

Giordano family would have to choose sides. And since Ryan and Nicholas were both Weres, I had assumed we would be firmly on the side of the furries.

Apparently, I was wrong, judging from the way Poppy clung to her tall, dark, and dead date.

"Daisy, you remember Liam," she said. She gazed adoringly into his eyes.

I cleared my throat. "Hello, Liam," I said. "Nice to see you." I'd met him briefly, but that had been months ago.

I tried to act casual as I scanned my sister's neck for bite marks.

"Daisy, Rose, it's nice to see you again," Liam replied. "Poppy talks about you all the time."

I wish I could say the same about him, I thought, then looked over at him guiltily. It wasn't his fault that Poppy never talked about him.

Could he read my thoughts? I didn't know that much about vampires. The vampire kids at school mostly kept to themselves, didn't bother anyone, and rarely dated anyone besides other vamps.

Some people said that vampires don't have a smell, but I could detect the faint odor of bitter violets and absinthe. It was an unaccountably attractive scent and seemed to be coming from Liam and the elder vampire.

The Vincent Price sound-alike broke away from the group and strode over to us.

"Grandfather," Liam said. "These are Poppy's sisters, Rose and Daisy. This is my grandfather, Count Vlad Dracul."

The vampire bowed low at the waist. "You are Daisy Giordano?" he asked me. "I have heard of you."

"Good things, I hope," I replied after a long pause. I was processing the fact that I was standing face-to-face with the legendary Dracula.

"You are involved with the Mendez pup," he said.

I bristled at his tone. And it gave me the creeps that he seemed to know an awful lot about my love life.

"I am dating Ryan Mendez, yes, but what business is it of yours?" I was being rude, and challenging a vampire was probably stupid, but he only raised an elegant eyebrow.

"Your loyalty is admirable," he said. "Let us hope it is not misplaced."

I sent Rose a message. *Poppy's dating Dracula's grandson? Great. Did you know about this?*

Of course not, she sent back.

The older vampire watched us intently until Poppy nudged me. "Cut it out," she whispered. "He can read minds."

"Most minds, my dear," Count Dracul replied. "But your sisters seem to be the exception."

I wondered if we really were the exception. I threw him a look, but his face remained expressionless. Maybe he was trying to throw us off.

Mr. Bone finally arrived, and everyone took a seat.

Vamps on one side and Weres on the other. The Weres were showing their teeth, and the vampires were out for blood. More people poured into the meeting, until it was standing-room only. Obviously, the news of the vampire/Were feud had spread. There weren't just council members attending tonight's meeting. It looked like every vampire and shifter for a hundred miles had made a trip to Nightshade.

Ryan hurried in and took a seat next to me. I was glad I'd saved a seat for him, just in case, although a particularly snippy Were rabbit had twitched her nose at me when I'd told her the seat was taken.

"Do you know what has everyone all riled up?" I asked him in a whisper.

Ryan cleared his throat. "A vampire teen was kidnapped a couple of days ago. He was rescued, but he was in the sun way too long and almost died."

"Why didn't you tell me this before?"

He shrugged. "I forgot," he said flatly.

"You forgot?" I said. He was making it very hard for me to hold on to my temper.

"Anything else you forgot to tell me?"

"Nothing I can think of," he said.

"Has anyone stopped to think that a kidnapping could be the work of the Scourge rather than some shifter payback?" Rose asked.

"It wasn't the Scourge," Ryan said. "The vampire said he

smelled wolf. And the kid in San Carlos? Bite marks all over the body. Let's face it—for once, it wasn't an evil Scourge plot. It was paranormals killing other paranormals."

Mr. Bone headed for the podium and banged on the gavel, but no one could hear him above the uproar. He finally resorted to switching to his much more intimidating look, a skeleton with a flaming skull.

That finally got the crowd's attention, and the shouting ceased almost immediately.

"The council believes that these incidents are not unrelated," he said.

There was a shout of agreement from the crowd.

"What are you going to do about it?" a Were growled.

Mr. Bone pounded on the gavel. "The council is taking this matter very seriously," he said. "We are using all our resources to find out who is responsible for these heinous acts."

Rose and I exchanged glances, and she sent a thought my way. *This is not good.*

There was another roar from one of the Weres, and then the room got so noisy that Mr. Bone had to bang on his gavel several times before he could be heard.

"Quiet. Quiet please!" he said. "If we all could just calm down?"

"Calm down?" Count Dracul said. "One of our young vampires was kidnapped from his home, taken to the beach, and left in the sun to burn."

"That was unfortunate," Mr. Bone said. "We are looking into it."

"There's no proof that the Weres did it," someone in the crowd yelled.

"We all know that this is in retaliation for the death of the young cub in San Carlos a few months ago. A terrible accident," the count replied.

"What about Elise Wilder? What kind of monster would attack an innocent girl?"

Chaos erupted, and for a moment I felt sure there was going to be a fight. But Mr. Bone went into his scary flaming-skull mode again, which reminded the crowd that he wasn't just a golf-loving mortician.

Count Dracul stood. "What motive would the vampires have for starting a war with the Weres? We have been at peace for over fifty years."

"Vampires aren't reasonable," a tall Were said. I didn't recognize her. "They only want one thing. Blood. And they don't care how they get it."

Liam jumped to his feet. "That's not true," he said. "We take blood only from willing donors."

I glanced at Poppy, wondering if she was Liam's latest "donor," but she met my gaze with a smile that told me nothing.

The meeting went downhill from there. It was obvious that neither the vampires nor the shifters were willing to listen to reason. Continuing the meeting was pointless.

"How are the Nightshade City Council members going to be impartial?" a tall pale vampire asked. "Mr. Bone, your son is a shifter."

"And several of our members are vampires," Mr. Bone replied. "For the last time, the council is looking into it. We have appointed a task force to investigate this matter. I hope the members of the task force meet with your approval."

"Who are they?" someone shouted.

"Liam Dracul, Nicholas Bone, and Chief Mendez will be working together to determine if these crimes were indeed paranormal hate crimes or if there is something else afoot," Mr. Bone said. "The task force will report directly to me, and I assure you, I will be able to maintain my impartiality."

Both sides seemed to calm down at the news. There was even a smattering of applause.

"In the meantime, I suggest you all go home," Mr. Bone said.

He managed, with a little help from Chief Mendez, to persuade everyone to go their separate ways.

Nicholas insisted on driving us home, but Poppy dug in her heels.

"I'm not going with you," she said stubbornly. "I came with Liam, and I'm leaving with him."

"Poppy," I said, "be reasonable."

"No harm will come to your sister," Count Dracul said. "I give you my word."

I raised an eyebrow. "Good."

He raised one right back at me. "Good."

Ryan gave me a quick kiss goodbye and then went to talk to his dad.

In the car, no one spoke for a minute, and then Nicholas said, "I can't believe you sassed Count Dracul, one of the oldest vampires in existence."

"I was worried about Poppy," I said. "That's the same guy she took to the Nightshade Through the Ages ball, but she never talks about him."

"Liam?" Nicholas said. "He seems all right."

Nicholas was a supernice guy, but I was surprised by his lack of animosity toward the vampires. I guess that was one of the reasons he was on the task force.

"You don't think a vampire attacked Elise?" I hazarded.

"I think someone wants us to believe that," he said. "But I want more evidence before I make my decision. The vampires and shifters have been at peace for over fifty years. I don't think a few incidents should jeopardize that."

Nicholas brought up a good point. It was nice to see he was taking his task force duties seriously.

"Who has a good reason to want the vampires and shifters to be at odds?" Rose said, and then answered her own question. "The Scourge."

Was Ryan right about the paranormal attacks? Or was the

Scourge trying to start a war between the vampires and shifters? Either way, this question remained: Would Nightshade survive a war between the vampires and shifters? The question bothered me for the rest of the night.

CHAPTER NINE

"The dinner party is this Saturday night," Mom announced at breakfast. On Friday.

The three of us immediately protested. "We already have other plans," Poppy said.

"Change them. You've been putting it off," she said. "And I heard what happened at the city council meeting last weekend. I expect everyone to be at the dinner."

Rose said, "But, Mom—"

Mom cut her off. "It's time to put a stop to this nonsense once and for all. I've already called all the pertinent adults. Seven sharp."

She made it clear that we didn't have any other choice.

"I'll talk to Ryan at school today."

"I'll have to trade shifts," Poppy said. Poppy worked part-time at the coffee shop on campus.

"Do that," Mom said. "Daisy, you're going to be late for school if you don't get a move on."

I gave Rose a beseeching look. "Can I bum a ride to school?"

"I need the car today," Poppy protested.

"Work it out, girls," Mom said. "I've got to get to work myself."

Poppy and Rose argued all the way to the car.

"I have class, Poppy," Rose said.

"And I have to get to work," she said.

"Uh, can you guys just drop me off before you head to campus?" I asked, but they ignored me.

"I want to drive," Poppy said. I rolled my eyes. It didn't take a psychic to see a tardy in my future.

I spotted Sam's VW convertible as it pulled into Sean's driveway, and I ran over. "Can I get a lift?" I asked her.

"Hop in," she said.

"I really appreciate it," I said. "Let me tell my sisters." But as we watched, they hopped into the car and took off without me.

I got into the back seat, then Sam honked the horn to let Sean know she was there. He came running out and we headed to school.

I wasn't sure how Mom expected her dinner guests to get along when her two older daughters couldn't seem to stop fighting.

The animosity seemed to be catching. At lunch a scuffle broke out in the cafeteria between two freshmen girls. One fighter ended up with a bloody nose, the other with a chipped tooth. Or should I say chipped fang.

Penny rushed up to me after my last class. "Did you hear?" she asked.

"Hear what?"

"San Carlos is canceling their prom." She lowered her voice. "Because of all the, you know, tension between the factions."

It was unfortunate, but I didn't get why Penny was in such a tizzy. Her boyfriend went to Nightshade too. We'd be fine. Unless . . .

"Did you hear anything about our prom getting canceled?" I asked.

"Shhh," she said. "Don't even say that out loud."

"But it's a possibility, isn't it?" I said. "That's why you're upset."

She nodded. "I overheard Principal Amador talking in the office," she confided. "No decision yet, but if anything else bad happens, it's *adios* senior prom."

"We're going to have to prevent that from happening," I said.

Penny smiled, but she still looked anxious. "Wouldn't it just be my luck if our prom gets canceled? I mean, I have a real boyfriend for the first time ever."

"If it gets canceled, we'll just have to get dressed up anyway," I said. I was trying to comfort myself as much as her.

My words did seem to make Penny feel better. "You're right," she said. "We can still get a limo, wear fancy dresses, the whole nine yards. No matter what."

"No matter what," I agreed, but secretly I wondered if the war between the Weres and vampires was escalating to a point of no return. Soon, it might not be safe to go out after dark in Nightshade.

Ryan and Sean had a baseball game on Saturday afternoon, and Sam and I went to watch our boyfriends play. When I got home, I could tell by the delicious smell that Dad was cooking for the dinner party that night. I followed my nose to the kitchen.

Grandma Giordano was sitting at the kitchen counter, sipping espresso.

"Grandma, I'm glad to see you," I said. "I've been meaning to call you."

She dipped biscotti into her coffee. "That's nice, dear," she said. "You're such a devoted granddaughter."

"Oh good, you're home," Dad said. "I could use your help." He was wearing his favorite apron. It said KISS THE COOK on it.

"What are we having for dinner?" I asked.

"It was tough figuring out what to serve vampires and werewolves," Dad said, "but I think I finally found the perfect menu."

"What can I do to help?"

"Do you want to make the dessert?" Dad asked. "Nothing fancy."

I grabbed another apron. "Do we have the ingredients for pie?"

"We probably have enough apples for a cobbler," Dad replied. "And there's plenty of vanilla ice cream in the freezer."

After I made the pie and put it in the oven, I went upstairs to change. When I came back down, I heard voices in the living room and went to see which of our guests had arrived.

I craned my neck to get a better view. Poppy was seated next to Liam, and on his other side was a dark-haired girl with a pixie cut and a bored expression.

Count Dracul was sitting on the love seat, but it was the woman sitting next to him who made me catch my breath. I had to look again to make sure I wasn't seeing things. Patrician features and long silver hair. Check. Loads of jewelry. Check. Freezing green eyes. Check. Circe Silvertongue was sitting in my living room. Her pet pig/enchanted ex Balthazar was lying at her feet.

My mother would be mortified if I picked a fight with a guest. I took a few calming breaths.

"Poppy," I said. I stood in the doorway, not trusting myself to get any closer to the sorceress. "Could I see you for a minute? In the kitchen?"

I stalked away before she could respond. She flew into the kitchen seconds after I did.

"What is she doing here?" I hissed. I tried to keep my voice as low as possible. Vampire hearing and all.

"Who?" she said, playing dumb. She knew exactly who I meant.

"Circe Silvertongue. Who do you think?"

She shrugged. "She's with Liam's grandfather," Poppy said. "He called and asked if he could bring someone. I couldn't say no."

"Couldn't you?"

"Daisy, you're being unreasonable," she replied.

"What is he doing with that sneaky witch anyway?" I asked.

"She's not a witch. She's a sorceress," she said.

"How can you sit there calmly sipping tea after what she did to Lily and poor Balthazar?" I kept my voice low, despite my urge to pull out my hair and scream.

"What did you want me to do?"

"We have to tell the council," I said.

"What would you like to tell the council?" The count stood where only seconds before there had been empty space.

We both stared at him, mouths agape.

"If you are referring to the presence of Circe Silvertongue in your lovely city, the council is fully aware," Count Dracul continued. "Her assistance was needed."

Mom came into the kitchen. "Is everything all right?" she asked.

"Everything's fine," I assured her.

Rose, Nicholas, Mr. Bone, and Ryan and his dad all trooped in.

"Look who I found on the doorstep," Rose said.

"We rang the doorbell, but no one answered," Ryan told me.

"Sorry," I said. "I was checking on the dessert." The pie! I'd completely forgotten about it. I grabbed a couple of potholders and yanked it out. It was a little crispy but it still looked edible.

When Dad called us all into dinner, Balthazar jumped up and trotted into the dining room. Ryan stayed behind with me while everyone else followed the pig out of the kitchen.

"Now that we don't have an audience, I can say hello properly," he said.

I kissed him. "Hello."

"That's it?" he complained. "One measly little kiss?"

"Sorry," I said. "Circe is here, and I'm in a foul mood because of it."

Dad called out, "Daisy, Ryan."

"We'd better get in there," I said, "before Dad comes looking for us."

Dad had moved our dining room table somewhere, then set up some folding tables into one long row and covered them with white linen tablecloths. Everyone was introduced, and then we took our chairs. Ryan sat next to me, and Grandma took the seat on the other side. The chief sat in between Ryan and Mr. Bone.

Count Dracul sat in the middle with Circe, and my sisters and their boyfriends sat at the other end with the dark-haired girl, who still hadn't uttered a word to anyone. Circe was close enough that I could talk to her. Not that I wanted to.

"This is my sister, Claudia," Liam said. He made the introductions around the table.

"Claudia? Really?" I whispered to Ryan. Claudia was the name of the minivamp in *Interview with a Vampire*.

"Claudia is a popular name with vampires," he replied softly.

Everyone seemed to be getting along well enough, although Claudia Dracul spent most of her time texting. She didn't touch her salad, not so much as a polite nibble. Even though vampires preferred blood, they *could* eat regular food.

"Claudia, how do you like Nightshade High?" I asked her, trying to be polite.

"It's not like home," she said.

"Where's home?" I asked.

She rolled her eyes. "Transylvania," she said, like it was obvious. Hey, how was I supposed to know what was real and what was myth?

"Are you dating anyone at school?" I didn't know what else to ask.

Her grandfather frowned.

"The boys at that school are so boring," she said, but I noticed she glanced at her grandfather to see if he was listening. He was.

"My granddaughter has not found the appropriate vampire companion," Count Dracul said.

Hmm. *Vampire* companion, huh? His attitude didn't bode well for Poppy's relationship. He'd been charming to my sister, but underneath all that charm, I could tell he wasn't happy with Liam's choice of girlfriend.

And apparently, what the count had told us about the council being in on Circe's return was true. Neither Mr. Bone nor Chief Mendez even batted an eye when they saw her.

"So how long have you known Circe was back?" I tried to make the question sound casual, but I was fuming. Why wasn't she in jail? Circe evidently picked up on my frustration.

"I have reformed," Circe said, "since I met Vlad."

It took me a second to realize she was talking about Count Dracul.

I forgot that I'd vowed to be polite and not upset my parents. "If you're so reformed, why are Lily and Balthazar still enchanted?"

Conversation stopped, and everyone turned to look at us.

"I do not have to answer to this child," Circe said. "Besides, she is heavy-handed with the garlic, and her sauces are pedestrian."

Count Dracul laid one hand gently upon Circe's arm, which seemed to calm her.

Grandma Giordano was so mad, her face was turning red. She opened her mouth, but nothing came out.

"Daisy is a very talented chef," Ryan objected. I grabbed his hand and squeezed it.

Then Poppy jumped to my defense. "Could you cook like Daisy when you were in high school?"

I shot Mom a pleading look. To be honest, I'd half expected things to deteriorate like this, but I didn't expect it to be over my cooking skills or lack thereof.

Mom said, "It's time for the next course. Daisy, can you help me bring it out?"

As soon as we got into the kitchen, I burst out, "Mom, I couldn't help it."

"I know," she said, "but it looked like you needed a minute to calm down."

When we returned with the soufflés, the conversation seemed to be about the weather.

I avoided Circe for the rest of the dinner, but I only picked at my food.

When everyone but me was done eating, Mom said, "Why don't we grownups take the coffee into the living room and let the kids get to know each other a little better."

"Are you feeling okay?" Ryan said in a low voice after they'd left. "You love your dad's soufflé."

"She makes me so mad," I said. "I'm going to find a way to free Lily with or without Circe Silvertongue."

I glanced up and saw that both Liam and Claudia were looking at me curiously.

"Sorry," I said. "Have you known Circe long?"

Claudia shrugged and returned her attention to her phone, but Liam answered me. "She and Grandfather met recently," he said, "and they hit it off. He finds her charming."

"Your grandfather had better be careful," I told him. "She turned one of her exes into a pig." I looked pointedly at Balthazar, who was curled up in the corner.

Poppy glared at me, but I ignored her.

Liam smiled as though my warning amused him. "My grandfather can take care of himself."

That was probably true. If Count Dracul, the stuff of myths and legends, couldn't handle Circe, there was no hope for the rest of us.

We joined the adults in the living room just as Mr. Bone was leaving.

"You're going already?" I said. "But we haven't had dessert yet." I was hoping to apply a little more pressure about Lily and Balthazar.

Chief Mendez stood up. "I've got to be going too," he said. "Thank you for a lovely evening. Ryan, I'll see you at home. Count. Circe." He gave them a brief nod, but I noticed he didn't shake hands with them.

Dad and Mom walked Mr. Bone and the chief out.

Rose and Nicholas were chatting with Grandma, and Liam and Poppy were making eyes at each other.

The count produced a thin cigarette case and said, "Filthy habit, I know, but once you've been smoking for two hundred years, it's hard to quit. I'll just step outside for a moment. Please excuse me." Circe followed him from the room.

As soon as her grandfather was out of sight, Claudia slipped out too. I wondered where she had gone, but I had bigger things to worry about. What was Circe up to?

"I'll clean up," I volunteered. I was pretty sure she and the count were in the backyard. The kitchen had the perfect vantage point.

Ryan cleared the dishes from the dining room while I rinsed the plates.

Circe and Count Dracul were sitting at the table on the back patio. The kitchen window was open, and I eavesdropped on their conversation as I loaded the dishwasher.

"But Vlad," she said, "I could not reverse the spell even if I wanted to."

He said something too low for me to hear.

"The pen," she replied. "I left it." If Circe had used the pen to cast a spell, she would want it where she could look at it every day and gloat. I was almost certain the pen she was talking about was the one I had seen at Wilder's Restaurant when I'd "won" those cooking lessons—the pen with Bam's initials on it.

"You could not find it?" the count asked.

"Perhaps, but the other item was"—she paused—"confiscated."

"Unfortunate," the count observed.

I suppressed a snort. I didn't believe anything she was telling him.

I couldn't pick up anything else she said, so I tried a little mind reading. The only words I picked up were *Balthazar* and *present*. I couldn't do it for long anyway, not without Circe catching me, so I went back to the old-fashioned kind of snooping. I moved closer.

"And there is no way to retrieve it."

"You're certain?" the count asked.

Poppy poked her head into the kitchen. "How's the dessert coming?"

I nearly dropped the plates.

"F-fine," I said. "Can you get the ice cream?"

"What are you so jumpy about?" she said, then looked over my shoulder. The count and Circe were clearly visible.

"Nothing," I said. I didn't sound convincing, even to myself.

"Daisy, I'm saying this for your own good," she said. "Stay away from Circe."

"Don't worry, I will," I told her. At least until I found that pen.

CHAPTER TEN

Seeing Circe back in Nightshade fueled my determination to free Lily and Balthazar.

The next morning, I called Bianca. "Hi, it's Daisy," I said. "Can I come by Wilder's?"

Bianca agreed to meet me before her shift at the restaurant.

As I maneuvered my car up the long drive, my thoughts went back to my junior prom, which had been held at the Wilder estate. The Scourge had done a total *Never Been Kissed* and had planted an agent who posed as a high school student. Prom night had been interesting, to say the least. I crossed my fingers that we weren't in for a repeat performance.

I waited for her in the empty dining room at Wilder's Restaurant. Her straight black hair swayed as she walked. There was still something feline in the way she moved, even when she was in human form.

She poured us a couple of sodas and then sat down.

"Thank you for agreeing to see me," I said, unsure where to start.

"Anytime," she said. "So, tell me where you're going to college."

I sighed. "I haven't heard from any colleges yet," I said.

"None? But isn't that a little unusual?"

"Maybe I just didn't get accepted anywhere," I said gloomily.

"But you would have received word either way, correct?" she prompted me. "Isn't it odd that you haven't heard one way or the other?"

Strangely, the thought cheered me up. Bianca was right. Colleges sent rejection letters as well as acceptance letters, and I had received neither. A mystery indeed.

"Now, I know you didn't come here for college advice. What can I help you with?" she asked.

"I've been looking into the disappearance of Mrs. Wilder's sister," I replied. "And I need your help."

"I'm not sure how I can help you," she said. "Circe and I weren't close or anything."

"Do you know where Circe stayed last time she was in Nightshade?"

"She stayed here, at the Wilders'," she replied. "In one of the guest rooms."

"I'm looking for something that Circe may have left here," I explained. "A pen engraved with Balthazar Merriweather's initials on it. Can I see her room?"

Bianca brushed her long black hair out of her eyes. "I can let you in there for about half an hour. That's it."

"That would be a big help," I said. "Thanks so much."

She led me up the stairs, past Mrs. Wilder's bedroom, which I'd actually been in once before under very strange circumstances.

"When did Mrs. Wilder buy this house?" I asked. I was only making idle conversation but was surprised by Bianca's answer.

"She grew up here. This was her parents' home."

"I just assumed that the mansion had belonged to Mrs. Wilder's husband," I replied. "I mean, it is called the *Wilder* mansion."

"It was the Varcol home before that," Bianca said. "Shortly after Mrs. Wilder married, her parents died and she inherited the estate. Eventually, people stopped calling it the Varcol mansion and started calling it the Wilder estate instead."

That was kind of cool. I was in the house where Lily had grown up. We went down the hallway and then took a different set of stairs up another flight. They were dark and narrow and had probably been used by servants in bygone days.

"Taking me the back way?" I asked.

"Yes," Bianca said flatly. "I don't want any of the staff to see you and start asking questions."

The thick carpet muffled the sound of our steps, and the entire house seemed still and silent. There was no noise from the restaurant in this part of the house. Bianca stopped in front of a door and took out a key and unlocked it. "This is where

Circe stayed," she said. She gestured to the adjacent room. "And that was Lily Varcol's bedroom."

"Really? Can I take a look?" I asked.

"Lily's room has been locked for years. Mrs. Wilder has the only key and allows no one entrance. She cleans this room with her own two hands twice a year without fail."

I was disappointed by the news. I would have loved to get a glimpse of where Lily had lived until she'd been banished to the jukebox.

Bianca opened the door to Circe's room. "I'll be back for you in half an hour," she said. "Not a minute longer."

Mrs. Wilder had given Circe a sumptuous room decorated in a sunny yellow. A white silk spread embroidered with violets covered the four-poster bed, and plump down pillows lined the headboard.

There was a delicate writing desk near the fireplace, and I decided that would be a logical place to hide a pen. I didn't find it there or under the bed. I checked in the large armoire, where I found a *Cooking with Circe* apron, but when I checked the pocket, there was nothing inside besides a couple of bad love poems in Circe's handwriting. I scoured the room but didn't find anything else even remotely interesting.

I approached the door that led to Lily's room. Bianca had said the room was always locked, but when I touched the door-knob, it opened without effort.

Lily's room must have been kept just as she'd left it. The room was decorated in a royal blue with a velvet coverlet and matching drapes surrounding the heavy teak bed. There were fresh flowers in a crystal vase on the nightstand, and it struck me that Mrs. Wilder must visit her sister's room considerably more than twice a year.

There was a long white nightgown crumpled on the floor and a jumble of perfume and makeup on the vanity. There was even a large carved box with a bunch of costume jewelry spilling carelessly out of it. At least, I hoped it was costume jewelry and not the real thing I removed each piece of jewelry as carefully as possible and tried to remember where everything had been.

I wandered aimlessly around the room. There were several sets of sheet music organized by song title on the window seat. Lily had liked music, it seemed, even before she'd been trapped in a jukebox.

Judging from the haphazard state of her room, Lily was somewhat disorganized, except for where her music was concerned. I crossed to the bed and looked under it. It was almost too dark to see anything, but then I caught a gleam of something out of the corner of my eye. My heartbeat accelerated, but it turned out to be a small flute.

The connecting door had been unlocked, which meant that it was possible Circe had been in the room too. I tried to think like a sorceress for a moment.

I heard voices in the hallway and jumped to my feet, then quickly slipped back into the other room through the connecting door.

"Time's up," Bianca said.

"Can I take a look at Circe's old office?" I asked. "Maybe there's a clue there."

"Of course," she replied. "And I wanted to introduce you to our new head chef anyway."

Bianca picked up on my hesitation. "Don't worry," she said. "He's nothing like Circe."

"Well, okay, if you don't think I'll be disturbing him," I said.

She led the way to the kitchen. "Pierre," she said to a round little man who kind of resembled Santa, if Santa had a fat black caterpillar of a mustache marching across his lip. "This is Daisy Giordano. She, er, interned here when Circe Silvertongue was head chef."

Interning was an interesting way to describe my time in the kitchen of Wilder's Restaurant. Shedding blood, sweat, and tears was another way to describe it.

He wiped his hand on his apron and then held it out to me. "The young detective? It's so nice to meet you. Bianca has been telling me we could use someone like you around here. I hear you are a talented chef yourself."

I shot a look at Bianca but managed to respond somewhat coherently. "Thank you." His cheery manner was the last thing I expected from an executive chef.

"Tell me, what are your plans for the summer?" he said.

"I don't have any yet," I said baldly, "although I work at Slim's part-time."

"A lovely establishment," he commented mildly. "I am thinking of starting a new cordon bleu program for talented college students."

"I'm not a college student," I said gloomily. "But I want to attend UC Nightshade in the fall."

"Excellent," Pierre said. "I was thinking of starting out small with a Saturday class. Perhaps a pastry class? Would you be interested?"

"Very much," I said.

"Pierre is one of the premiere pastry chefs in the United States," Bianca said.

He blushed modestly and waved away her praise, then clapped his hands together. "It is settled, then. I will contact you once the details are finalized."

"Do you mind if we take a look at Circe's old office?" Bianca asked. "Daisy is investigating something related to Circe and believes Circe may have left something there that would be beneficial."

He nodded. "I prefer to use the other office," he said. "That one still stinks of bad magic. I did pack up her things. The box is on the desk. Feel free to look through it."

Bianca escorted me to the office and then excused herself, saying her shift was starting soon and she needed to change.

I dug through the contents of the box. I found a couple of recipes in Circe's handwriting, an empty bottle of perfume, and a UC Nightshade mug Circe had been using to hold her pens and pencils. I'd almost given up hope when I spotted a familiar black pen.

My heart beat faster as I turned it over to look for the initials. BM. Success! I put the pen in my pocket and replaced the rest of her stuff before sealing the box back up.

I went through the kitchen and couldn't help but notice that the kitchen staff were all smiling, a marked contrast to the atmosphere when Circe had been in charge

Pierre was showing something to the sous chef when I walked by, but he stopped what he was doing and said, "Daisy! Daisy, please wait. I have something for you."

I stopped and waited for him. He came huffing up and presented me with a pink pastry box.

"For you and your family," he said. "I hope you enjoy these. And please think about my class."

"I will," I promised him. I smiled and said goodbye, feeling more cheerful than I had in ages. I'd found Balthazar's pen and gotten a gift of delicious-smelling baked goods. A good day of detecting.

On the drive home, a thought struck me.

Rose had brought up the very real possibility that the

Scourge was responsible for the attacks. Its members hated vampires and shifters equally and would have no qualms about killing as many paranormals as they could.

There had to be someone in charge of that heinous organization, which was the evil equivalent of the Nightshade City Council. The Scourge was behind my father's kidnapping. Did my dad know something?

Dad was being all writer-crazy about his book and refused to talk about it. We'd tiptoed around him ever since his return. Sure, he'd told the council what he remembered, but that had been when he first came home. Some of his memories were coming back. Maybe he had remembered something and written it down, not thinking it was anything important?

I'd promised Wolfie that I would look into Elise's attack. I had pastries and a good reason to grill Dad.

I got lucky. He was the only one home when I got back from the restaurant.

"Where is everyone?" I asked.

His laptop was open on the kitchen counter, but he reached over, hit Save, and then closed it. He obviously didn't want me to read whatever he was working on.

"Rose is out with Nicholas, and your mom is working."

"Where's Poppy?" I didn't want my chatty sister coming in and interrupting my interrogation.

"Work, I think."

Or maybe she's with Liam, giving blood, I couldn't help thinking.

"Would you like one?" I asked. I opened the pink box and waved it in front of him enticingly.

He reached in and snagged a chocolate-dipped macaroon.

"Dad, can I ask you something?"

"You just did," he said. He took another bite.

"Ha ha, very funny," I replied. "I'm serious."

"Okay, shoot."

I didn't know how to start. "Have another one. This one is a raspberry-filled cookie."

"Daisy, you know you can ask me anything," he said. "You don't have to bribe me with cookies."

"You know about Elise Wilder's attack," I said. "And the others."

He nodded.

"Rose thinks that it's not as simple as vampires versus shifters," I said. "She thinks that the Scourge is behind it."

"She has a good head on her shoulders," Dad said.

"Have you remembered anything about your captivity?" I asked him. "Anything new, I mean?"

He crossed his arms over his chest, a sure sign he didn't want to talk about it.

"It's important," I said.

He didn't say anything but took a long, shaky breath. "I keep hearing the voices in my head."

"Who?" I said, but I knew the answer.

90

"Her. I hear the sound in my dreams, but when I wake up, it's gone. I can't place it."

"It's okay, Dad," I said. I felt horrible about his reaction. "Maybe it's better if you don't remember."

"I would love to remember," he replied. "I would love to help catch the people who kept me away from my family for so long."

"So, there are no details about your kidnappers in the book?" I asked.

He hesitated. "There is one thing," he finally said. "But I don't think it's important."

"You never know," I told him.

"There were two of them giving orders," he said. "A man and a woman. They were always arguing." My dad almost seemed to be talking to himself.

"About what?" I didn't want to break his concentration, but the question escaped from me.

"Me. Nightshade. And something else." Dad's voice sounded far away. "The woman's voice. It was garbled."

"Garbled? Like she used a voice-modification machine?"

"No," he replied. "I think I was drugged. My vision and thinking were distorted. I felt out of it. I don't remember much about that night. I was working. Someone offered me a drink, and after that . . ."

"After that what?" I asked.

"I don't know," he replied. "I don't know."

His voice was rising and his hands were shaking. It was time to stop asking him questions.

"It's okay, Dad," I soothed. "Why don't we make some hot chocolate and pop in a movie?"

He exhaled slowly. "Hot chocolate sounds good."

As we heated up the milk, I vowed that I would eventually find out who had done so much harm to my father's psyche. And I'd make them pay. Somehow.

CHAPTER ELEVEN

A few days later, my cell phone buzzed in my backpack. I dug it out but didn't recognize the number.

"Hello?"

"Daisy, it's Natalie. I thought you'd want to know what I learned about, er, what you asked me about. Can you meet me later?"

She must have been somewhere very public because she was being deliberately vague.

"I found out some stuff too," I said.

"I've got to get to class now," she replied. "But maybe we can meet later? My last class ends at four."

We agreed to meet at Slim's and hung up.

"Want to come with me?" I asked Sam.

When I told her what I was trying to find out, she was all for tagging along.

Natalie was already there when Sam and I arrived. Sometimes I felt like I practically lived at Slim's, but when Natalie suggested it, I couldn't say no. She wanted to spend time with Slim and she was doing me a favor. Besides, I needed to check in with Lil.

I slid into the booth where Natalie was sitting. I almost sat on Slim, but the laughter on Natalie's face gave it away in time and I managed to catch myself.

"Sorry, Slim," I said. "I didn't see you there."

Natalie giggled and I made a face at her.

"Time for me to get back to the kitchen," Slim said. "Can I get you anything?"

"I'd love an order of fries when you get a chance," I said.

"Make that two," Sam said.

"Do you want anything, babe?" he asked Natalie.

"Not anything from the kitchen," she teased. I didn't think it was possible to watch an invisible man blush, but I had no doubt that's what Slim was doing.

Natalie's giggles followed him all the way to the kitchen.

After she finally stopped laughing, she turned to me and said, "Okay, this is what I found out."

She pulled a large notebook out of her bag and flipped through it until she found the page she was looking for. "I finally found a precedent for this situation. Back in 1815, a witch trapped her rival in a grandfather clock. But the rival's coven managed to undo the spell."

"That's great news!" I said. "Do you think you'll be able to break the spell on Lily and Bam? What do we need to make it happen?"

"If I have the gist of it, it helps to know the emotion behind the act. You know, greed, gluttony."

"Jealousy?" I asked.

"Why, yes," she said. "Why do you mention that emotion in particular?"

"Circe had a thing for Balthazar Merriweather, but he only had eyes for Lily Varcol."

"We don't have anything better to go on," she said.

"Actually, we do," I said. I filled her in on the conversation I'd overheard between Circe and the count.

Sam, who had been completely silent during our conversation, finally spoke up. "What else do we need?"

"We need the items she used to enchant them," Natalie said. "And the presence of all enchanted parties, of course."

I was regretting my promise to Lil, just a tiny bit. It seemed like a tall order, especially since Circe wasn't cooperating and she was unlikely to hand over her precious pig. I glanced over at Lil. I hoped she hadn't heard our conversation. It wouldn't help to upset her any more than she already was.

"Circe said the second item had been confiscated," I said.

"Do you think she was telling the truth?" Sam asked.

"Maybe," I said. "She didn't know I was listening in. At least, I don't think she did."

Slim came back with the fries and a pitcher of ice water with three glasses. "Natalie gets dehydrated easily," he said.

"He takes such good care of me," she cooed. I was happy for them.

After he left, we continued our conversation.

"What happens to Lily and Balthazar?" I said. "Assuming we find the objects and reverse the spell?"

Natalie looked startled. "They go back to being human."

"Lily's been trapped in the jukebox for a long time," I pointed out. "And Balthazar has been a pig for just as long. Mrs. Wilder is Lily's younger sister and she's quite—"

"Ancient?" Sam said.

I gave her a dirty look. "Elderly," I continued. "It seems tragic that even if we do restore them to their human forms, they—"

"Might not survive the reunion?" Sam finished my sentence. "That doesn't seem fair."

We turned to Natalie with pleading looks.

She sighed. "Don't get your hopes up," she said. "But I'll see what I can find out about that too."

"I owe you one," I said. "That reminds me. Do you have any time to tutor a young witch? Her parents are norms, so she doesn't really have any family information to help her out."

"I'm still an intermediate myself, so I don't know how much help I'd be," Natalie said.

"She's kind of a loose cannon," I replied. "Any help you could give her would be appreciated."

"Who is it, if you don't mind my asking?" Natalie said.

"Penny Edwards," I said. I watched her, dreading the no that I was sure was forming on her lips.

But Natalie surprised me. "Okay, I'll do it. Give me her number and I'll set something up."

I looked at Sam. "I don't have Penny's cell number."

She pulled out her cell phone and scribbled the numbers down on a paper napkin and handed it to Natalie. "Don't feel bad if you want to wring her neck half the time," Sam said. "We all do. But Penny's not so bad once you get to know her."

Natalie stuck the number in her bag. "Look, I've got to go. Slim and I have plans."

Slim was turning the Open sign to Closed, which shocked me. "I can stay and cook if he needs me," I offered, but Natalie shook her head.

"He's closing the restaurant for a private party," she said. "Just the two of us."

"Thanks for your help, Natalie. I'll just say goodbye to Lil."

I was startled when Lil broke into "Marry Me" by Train. "Oh," I said. "*Oh!*" I repeated as the light dawned. "Come on, Sam, let's go." I took her by the arm and propelled her out the door.

"What's your hurry?" she said as the door closed behind us.

"I think Slim is going to propose to Natalie," I whispered.

"He is?" she replied. "That's so romantic. Are you sure?"

"Lil seems to think so. And have you ever known Slim to close the diner?" I said. "And besides, I saw this little black velvet box in his office the other day."

"Did you open it?" Sam asked.

"Of course not," I said. "But I'm almost sure it's an engagement ring. He's crazy about Natalie."

"That's a big step," Sam said. "Do you ever think about it?"

"Getting married?" I asked. "We're way too young to even think about marriage."

"I know," she said. "But what about someday?"

I shrugged. "Maybe someday. Right now, I just want to make it through graduation."

At the time, I had no idea just how much of a challenge that was going to be.

CHAPTER TWELVE

Saturday morning meant an early shift at Slim's. Flo had been coming in later and later. She finally explained with a giggle that she wanted to sleep in on the weekends. I pretended it was because she was up late watching her musician boyfriend's gigs and blocked all other thoughts from my mind.

After my shift ended, I went home and baked sugar cookies. I was kicking back in the family room, waiting for the cookies to cool, when I got a text message from Sam. *Look out your front window.*

I went to the window and looked out. At first I didn't see anything, but I finally realized what Sam was talking about and fully appreciated the view.

Ryan was on the front lawn, shirtless, tossing a football back and forth with Sean.

Since it was hot out, I was wearing a scruffy old pair of shorts and a T-shirt splattered with dried paint. I rushed upstairs to change into my cutest shorts and a bright yellow top and made a beeline for my boyfriend.

The guys were still playing football, but I saw Samantha lolling on a chaise lounge in front of the Walshes' house, so I went on over. She was wearing a bikini top and shorts.

"Hey, what's going on?"

"Getting a little sun before prom," she said.

"You're turning pink," I said. "You'd better flip over."

"Ryan was coming over to see you when Sean grabbed him for a game," she said. "They've been at it for an hour and I'm bored."

"And you knew the sight of my boyfriend would bring me out of the house," I said. "Why didn't you just ring the bell?"

"I didn't feel like getting up," she confessed with a giggle. There was a pitcher of lemonade and glasses on a stand beside her. "Want a glass?"

I nodded. She reached for a small silver bucket of ice and plunked a few cubes in a glass before pouring the lemonade.

The guys jogged over, and my boyfriend wrapped his slightly sweaty arms around me.

"Hey, babe," Ryan said. He nuzzled my neck. "You smell good."

"Vanilla," I said. "I was baking cookies."

"Break some of those bad boys out," Sean said.

I went to the house and came back with a plate of cookies.

I handed Ryan and Sean cookies and then waved one in front of Sam's face. She refused it.

Sean's little sister Katie came running out, her lips and hands stained a bright red. For a second, I thought it was blood, but then I realized she had been eating strawberries.

She was followed closely behind by one of his other sisters, Jessica I think. Sean had seven sisters, and it was sometimes hard to keep track of who was who. Katie was the youngest and Samantha's favorite. Jessica was not.

Jessica didn't resemble her sisters. The others looked like Katie, strawberry blond curls and big blue eyes, but Jessica had long, straight auburn hair, steel gray eyes, and a chip on her shoulder. She'd be starting Nightshade High after we graduated.

"Katie, let me wipe off your face," Sam said.

"I'll do it," Jessica snapped.

There was a tense moment while the two girls glared at each other, until Samantha finally caved in.

"Fine," she said. She handed Jessica the wet cloth.

"I want Sam to do it," Katie protested.

Jessica gave in and handed Sam the cloth, but not without giving her a dirty look first.

Ryan gave me a quick kiss. "Thanks for the cookies," he said. He tossed the football at Sean and they went back to their game.

"I need your help with something," Samantha said. "It won't take up much of your time."

"What?" I said cautiously.

"Just feeding some yearbook volunteers on Monday," she replied. "You can do that in your sleep."

"I do have a couple of mysteries to solve," I pointed out.

"Please, Daisy," she said. "I want everything to be perfect. It's my last hurrah as an organizer."

Jessica snorted, then it was Samantha's turn to send Jessica a dirty look. I wondered what was up between the two of them. They obviously didn't get along well, although Katie clearly loved Sam.

Jessica led Katie back into the house, and I took the opportunity to grill Sam.

"What's the deal with you and Jessica?" I asked.

"She can't stand me," Sam replied. "Or more accurately, she can't stand it that Katie prefers me to her."

"Katie does adore you," I observed. "But you hang out with all of Sean's sisters."

Samantha shrugged. "True, but Katie and I are really close. Jessica is convinced that Sean and I are going to break up when he leaves for college and then Katie will be heartbroken."

"A lot of couples do break up after high school," I said, verbalizing my own fear.

"Sean and I are solid," she said. She picked up on my own doubt. "Don't worry. You and Ryan will be fine."

I sat in the chaise next to her, and we watched the guys play. I thought about what she had said. Would Ryan and I be fine? Or would our relationship be a casualty of distance and diverging interests?

The sun was setting by the time the guys finally got tired and plopped down next to us.

"Hey, have you seen Wolfie in school lately?" I asked them.

"He was out all last week," Ryan said. "Maybe his parents finally shipped him off to military school or something."

"Wolfie probably went off in a huff and will slink back with his tail between his legs," Sean suggested.

"Maybe," I said.

He shrugged. "Things are weird right now."

I sat there running over the options. If Wolfie had disappeared and it got out, there was no telling what the Weres would do. They'd blame the vampires for sure.

Monday, I wandered through the halls of school looking for Wolfgang. Instead, I ran into Penny. "Have you seen Wolfgang Paxton today?" I asked her.

"Why would you want to talk to him?" she asked.

"I wanted to ask him how Elise is doing," I explained.

"I haven't heard much about Elise, but you won't find Wolfie mooning around," she said.

"What?"

"Rumor has it—" She stopped, then smiled sheepishly. "I promised Tyler I'd stop gossiping so much."

Penny must be in love to make a promise like that.

"What did you hear?" I asked. "I could really use a lead on this case."

She lowered her voice. "I heard he's lying low because people aren't happy about who he's dating."

I gaped at her. "What people? Who is he dating? And how do you know all this?"

She giggled. "I still hear things the old-fashioned way. Besides, I'm a witch, remember?"

"Which reminds me," I said. I kept my voice low too. "Natalie Mason will be giving you a call. She's decided to take you under her wing and show you a few spells."

Penny gave an earsplitting squeal of delight. "Thanks, Daisy. You're the best." Her boyfriend, Tyler, came up before I could ask her anything else about Wolfgang.

"Yearbook meeting at Sean's today after school," Samantha said at lunch. "Daisy, you're cooking. I'll buy the supplies, so give me a list."

"Okay, but I'm only making simple stuff," I said.

Sam had volunteered a bunch of her core minions to help with the yearbook staff's "most likely to" picks.

We met at Sean's house. I'm not sure his parents knew

what they were getting themselves into by agreeing to let us meet there, but then again, Sam and Sean had been dating a long time.

Sam and I were in the kitchen. She was watching while I warmed up the buttermilk chicken bites. I'd made coleslaw by cheating a little and using my powers, then whipped up a quick spicy barbeque dip for the chicken. She had bought bakery cookies as big as my fist, but I wasn't sure if we had enough food.

Sam grabbed a toothpick and snagged one of the chicken bites. "These are good," she said through a mouthful of food. There was a time when all Samantha ate was an occasional granola bar, but since we'd been hanging out again, she was eating more regularly.

"I had Sean pick up some strawberries," she said. "I thought you could make those little shortcake thingies."

"Sam, everyone will be here in half an hour," I said, exasperated. "I have to run home and get the ingredients."

"I have everything you need," she replied.

I shot her a suspicious look, but she smiled serenely.

"I hope so." I went to the fridge and got out the ingredients. "I'd better get the shortcakes in the oven before everyone else gets here."

The doorbell rang, and Sam went to answer it while I mixed up the shortcakes and put them into the oven.

I had my back to the door when someone came up behind me and put his arms around me.

"Hi, Ryan," I said.

"How did you know it was me?" he asked.

I turned in his arms and gave him a quick kiss on the lips. "I just knew. I am psychic, after all."

"But you can't read my mind, can you?" He sounded nervous.

"I'll never tell," I said.

He gave me a little peck on the ear.

"Do you realize that this could be the last time you kiss my ear?" I said.

"I certainly hope not," he said. He kissed me again.

"I mean in this house," I said. "It's all ending, Ryan."

"Not everything," he said. "We'll never end."

"You don't know that," I replied. "You'll be hundreds of miles away. What if you meet someone else and break up with me?"

"I won't," he said firmly. "Don't you know? There's no one for me but you."

Despite my moodiness, his words brought a smile to my face.

"I know," I said. "And I feel the same way."

"So there will be no more talk of breaking up," Ryan said.

"Okay," I said. I grabbed his hand and swung it in the air, suddenly feeling happy for the first time in days.

"Besides, you and Sam are going to drive down to see one of our games, right?"

"As many as we can," I said. "I can't wait to see you in that Anteaters uniform."

People started to arrive for the meeting, so Ryan helped me finish getting the food into serving bowls and grabbed the paper plates and plastic cutlery.

"Where does Sam want all this stuff?" he asked.

"There are folding tables and chairs set up in the back-yard," I replied.

We carried the food to the backyard and put it in the designated location near a cooler full of sodas.

A bunch of kids from school were already sitting at the tables, but they jumped up as soon as they saw the food. We filled our plates and sat at a table with Sean, Sam, and Rachel and Jordan.

Sam started the meeting. "Okay, let's get started, everyone. First on the agenda, who should be on the ballot for most likely to succeed?"

There was a chorus of boos from the crowd. "Can't we do something more original?" Lilah Porter said.

"Like what?" Sam challenged her.

"Well, let's face it," Lilah said. "Everyone knows that Nightshade isn't like other schools. Why not pick categories that fit who we really are?"

"I nominate Lilah for best swimmer," Reese said.

"How about best transformation?" Jordan suggested.

"Most likely to howl at the moon?" someone else shouted.

"Best cape," another voice said.

"Furriest and foxiest," Penny said. "I'm talking to you, Ryan Mendez."

Everyone laughed at that.

While Sam spent the rest of the time arbitrarily assigning people to the tasks for yearbook, I had fun. My only job was to make sure there was enough food to go around.

A couple of people even asked me for the recipe for my buttermilk chicken bites.

When the meeting ended, Lilah came up to me as I was picking up soda cans to put in the recycling bin. She glanced over her shoulder, which meant that she didn't want to be overheard.

"Hey, Daisy, is Samantha okay?"

"A little bossy sometimes, but she has a good heart," I tossed out without thinking.

"No, I mean about her father," she said.

"What about her father?"

"I didn't want to say anything," she said.

"You're worried or you wouldn't say anything," I replied. Lilah wasn't the type to spread gossip.

"I heard there's some issue with his tenure at the university. And that his publisher didn't buy his new book," she said. "They even canceled his book tour."

"That can't be true," I said. "He's gone all the time."

"Well, whatever he's doing, he's not touring," she said.

If Mr. Devereaux wasn't off doing publicity, what was he up to? And why was he lying about it to everyone?

CHAPTER THIRTEEN

It was only Tuesday, but I already felt like the week had gone on forever. I was ready for a quiet evening at home involving homework, a little light reading, and then bed. My evening didn't turn out that way.

"I heard Elise is coming home," Ryan said when we met in front of the vending machines after third period. "There's going to be a little welcome home party at the Wilders' tonight."

"What time?" I said. "I could bake a cake."

Ryan looked at his feet. "I'm sorry, Daisy," he said. "This is a shifters-only party."

I stared at him, unable to believe what I'd just heard. "What? Are you serious?"

He burst out laughing. "I was just kidding!"

"It's not funny," I said. "There's been enough of that kind of stuff going on."

He stopped laughing. "I didn't mean to hurt your feelings."

"Well, you did," I said. The tension in Nightshade was getting to me, and I was taking it out on Ryan. I took a deep, calming breath. "Now, do I have time to bake a cake or not?" I asked.

"It's not until seven," he said. "You have plenty of time. I can take you to the store right after school if you need me to."

I couldn't stay mad at him. "I think I already have everything I need at home, but thanks for the offer."

When I got home, I whipped up a quick three-layer cake and started the frosting while the cake baked. After the layers had cooled, I used fresh raspberries and whipping cream as a filling and topped it off with Grandma's coconut frosting.

The party was being held in the Wilders' private quarters. When Ryan and I arrived, Bianca was putting up a welcome home banner in the living room, which was huge. There was a large stone fireplace at one end and a baby grand piano at the other. A group of kids from Nightshade High were milling around, and I noticed a few people I'd worked with when I'd had cooking lessons from Circe.

Elise came in with Mrs. Wilder a few minutes later, and a bunch of kids immediately surrounded her.

"Let her sit down first," Bianca said. She took Elise's arm and guided her to an overstuffed chair. Mrs. Wilder sat on a spindly little gilded chair that looked uncomfortable, but it was next to her granddaughter, so she seemed happy.

An antique buffet was lined with china and gold cutlery, and another table held chafing dishes full of delicious-smelling food.

I saw Pierre and remembered that he was a world-class

pastry chef. I immediately felt foolish that I had brought a cake from home.

But he made me feel better when he rushed over and took the cake container from me. "Daisy, how thoughtful of you. I can't wait to have a piece of your handiwork." He put the cake on the table and removed the cover.

I squirmed as he observed the cake from all angles. "Very nice," he said. "And the frosting? You made it yourself?"

I nodded. "It's an old family recipe."

"Very nice," he repeated.

"Thanks." Pierre was making me blush.

"Don't forget about my pastry class," he said. "The first class is at the end of June."

"I won't," I promised.

Chief Mendez and Officer Denton stopped by, but they didn't stay long. They said hello to Elise and Mrs. Wilder and then went into a corner and conversed briefly with Bane.

I nudged Ryan. "What was that all about?" I asked.

He shrugged. "I didn't know Dad was going to be here either. Probably something to do with the case."

"Maybe," I said. But what was so important that they had to track Bane down at Elise's welcome home party?

"I'm going to go say hi to my dad before he leaves," Ryan said.

"I'll go say hi to Elise," I said. "It looks like the crowd has dwindled a bit."

I lucked out. She was alone when I crossed over to her.

"Hi, Elise," I said. "Welcome home."

"Daisy, thank you so much," she said. "You saved me. If I can ever repay you, just say the word."

"You don't need to repay me," I told her. "But you could clear something up for me. I thought I heard you say 'vamps' when I found you."

She shook her head and then gestured for me to lean in. "The chief asked me not to say anything, but I can tell you. I was trying to say something else entirely."

"What were you trying to say?"

"Trap," she said. "I was trying to say it was a trap."

"What? I can't believe I was so far off."

"I can't believe I fell for the lost-kitten routine," she replied.

"You mean, some guy came up to you and asked you for your help finding a kitten?"

She nodded.

"Elise, that's the oldest trick in the book," I said. "Creepy guys have tried that for ages."

"I know," she said. "But it wasn't a guy. And it wasn't a vampire. It was a woman."

"Have you ever seen her before?" I asked.

"No, but she had this scar or something on her face."

"Could it have been a birthmark?" I wondered if it could possibly be the woman who had shown up at the Devereaux's door.

She nodded again. "Maybe." She put one hand to her throat.

"Let me get you some tea," I said. There was about every option under the sun for beverages. When I went to the buffet line, I found hot water and about fifty gourmet tea bags. I fixed her tea and headed straight back to her.

"This should help soothe your throat a little," I said. Elise was wearing a high-necked shirt that covered most of her injury, but I couldn't help wondering how bad the scar was.

"One last thing. I could use a little information about your grandmother's sister Lily."

When she frowned, I said, "I've kept my promise not to bother your grandmother with this, but I think I know where Lily is. I just need a couple of questions answered."

She nodded.

"Do you know if your grandmother has anything of Lily's that might have been a gift from her fiancé?"

"He was the heir to a big department store," she said. "Grandmother said he gave Lily lots of gifts."

That didn't narrow it down much.

"Is there anything specific you can think of?"

She shook her head. "Sorry."

"I borrowed a dress for the Nightshade Through the Ages ball," I said. "Your grandmother said it belonged to Lily. Do you mind if I borrow it again? Just for a day or two?"

"It's in storage," she said. "Go ahead and take it. Bianca can help you find it." She waved to Bianca and gave her instructions.

When I came back with the dress, I ran into Bane in the hallway.

"Hi, Bane," I said.

He hesitated when he saw me. "Daisy," he said.

His clothes looked like he'd slept in them, and there was three days' growth of hair on his face, which for a Were was a considerable amount.

"Is everything okay?" I asked, alarmed by his appearance.

"I'm fine," he said. "I just haven't been sleeping much. I'll catch up on my sleep now that Elise is home."

"How's Wolfgang? He wasn't in school last week. This week either."

"Uh, yeah," he said. "He's sick."

"Is that why he isn't here?" I asked.

I was picking up a weird vibe from Bane.

"I could come by with tomorrow's homework," I said.

"No!" Bane said. "He's, uh, still contagious."

I met his eyes. "If Wolfgang is in some sort of trouble, I can help."

That got a reaction, I was sure of it. But Bane still didn't tell me what was really going on.

"Listen, I can't talk right now," he replied. "I need to get back to Elise."

He took off, practically running to get away from my questions. Interesting.

Bane was lying to me about Wolfgang. But why? He didn't want me to go to their house? Why? Because Wolfgang wasn't there? Then where was he?

The idea of adding a lost Were to my list of mysteries to solve didn't exactly thrill me, but I couldn't ignore my intuition. Wolfie was in trouble. He was a pain, but he was our pain.

CHAPTER FOURTEEN

That Saturday night, Ryan and I had the house to ourselves, but even kissing my boyfriend didn't distract me.

"Doesn't the council care about Lily? She's stuck in the jukebox forever unless we find a way to break that spell."

Impatient, I decided to find Circe myself and confront her. Ryan tried to talk me out of it.

"How are you going to find her?" he said.

"Your dad didn't mention where she is staying?" I asked him.

"Nope," he replied. "I've told you everything I know."

Poppy walked in as I was ranting. "What's wrong?" she asked. "You look mad."

"I am mad," I said. "I still haven't freed Lily, and the council is just letting Circe walk right back into Nightshade like she didn't do a thing wrong. I want to confront Circe."

Poppy hesitated for a second. "Liam would kill me if he knew I was telling you this—"

"Then don't," I said. "I don't want to lose a sister."

She laughed at me. "Not literally," she said. "Liam wouldn't hurt a fly. You've got to get past the whole vampire thing."

"I'll try," I said. "I just don't want you to get hurt."

"I know." She gave me a little hug. "But you're in greater danger than I am of getting hurt if you're going to confront Circe. Although, I know the count will try to keep her under control. Liam and I saw him earlier, and he told us he's having a late dinner with Circe tonight."

"Where?"

She shrugged. "I don't know, but the count is renting out the old Mason place from Natalie. Start there."

I knew exactly where the Mason house was, but I hadn't known it had been rented out. After her grandmother died, Natalie moved in with Slim, but she still tended to her grandma's garden. I'd just bought a pumpkin from her there in the fall.

"I won't be home too late," I said. "But just in case, can you—"

"Cover for you? Sure."

Ryan followed me out to the car.

"I'm going with or without you," I warned him.

"C'mon, I'll drive," he said. He opened the passenger door of his car and waited for me to get settled before he got in and fired up the engine.

Ryan parked across the street from the Mason house, about a block down from it, and killed the engine.

I must have fallen asleep, because I woke with a start to the sound of someone's car starting. An expensive black sports car pulled out of the driveway. We followed Count Dracul as he sped toward San Carlos.

We stayed as far back as we could and hoped that he wouldn't spot us. With one look at the clock, I kissed my curfew goodbye and we continued to follow him.

Count Dracul eventually pulled into San Carlos's only five-star hotel, which only confirmed Poppy's tip that he was meeting Circe. She had expensive tastes. He left his car with the valet, while Ryan parked on the main street.

As I watched the count enter the hotel, my cell buzzed and I jumped. It was a text from Poppy checking to see if I was okay. I sent a quick message back.

Circe was keeping a low profile, but for a criminal, she was pretty easy to find.

Ryan and I followed the count, but when he got on the elevator, we were stymied for a few seconds.

"What now?" Ryan said.

"Watch the light. He was the only one in the elevator. Maybe we can tell what floor the elevator stops at."

"Twelve," Ryan said. "He got off on twelve."

We took the next elevator and got off on the twelfth floor.

The hallway was deserted.

"We can't knock on every door," Ryan pointed out.

"Maybe we won't have to," I said. I stopped and closed my eyes. After about a minute, I couldn't pick up any thoughts, but I was pretty sure I could hear the count's voice. He sounded aggravated. He had to be talking to Circe.

I moved along the hallway until I came to the door where the voices were the loudest.

"I think this is it," I told Ryan.

He knocked on the door.

I heard Wolfgang Paxton on the other side. "Finally! Room service. I'm starving."

But it was Circe who opened the door. Her eyes gleamed like green glass, and I remembered that I was confronting a powerful sorceress. "Daisy Giordano," she said. She said my name the way other people said "snake" or "spider" or maybe "shower scum."

"Let them in," Count Dracul said. "And quickly, before anyone sees."

We stepped into a large suite decorated in a modern style, all hard edges and black and white with splashes of red. A long red couch faced what I assumed were the windows, but it was hard to tell, because the drapes were closed tight. The count and Circe were seated at a small table. Circe had her pet pig with her, of course. An older woman and a younger girl were seated on the red couch but Wolfie was nowhere to be seen.

I reached over and petted Balthazar. "I know who he really is, you know," I said. "And I have the dress." I knew the dress wasn't the key to freeing Lily and Balthazar. I was fishing for information.

"A dress?" Circe scoffed. "That's the best you could come up with? Hardly a symbol of true love."

"What item did you use?" I persisted.

Circe laughed in my face. For quite some time. When she finally stopped cackling, she said, "Do not meddle in things of which you know nothing, little Giordano," she said. "Or I might not be so pleasant next time."

Only a healthy sense of self-preservation prevented my reply.

Ryan's pacing brought him near the two strangers, and the older woman jumped to her feet.

I knew I'd heard Wolfie's voice, and there was something about the way the woman moved. Like *he* wasn't used to walking in heels.

"Wolfie, is that you?" I asked. It was hard to tell, because most of his body was covered by a long blond wig, a flowing caftan thing he'd probably borrowed from Circe, and copious amounts of costume jewelry.

"I'm afraid you have the wrong person, young lady," he said in a high, thin voice.

"Wolfie, I know it's you," I said. "I'd recognize that obnoxious tone anywhere."

"I'm afraid you are quite mistaken," Circe said from behind me. "This is my cousin Mildred." There was a blast of cold air at my back, which told me she was in danger of losing her temper.

"So sorry," I said. I wasn't sorry at all. I could see Wolfgang's pleading eyes under the disguise.

The younger woman snickered and then stood. She was dressed like a dowdy tourist in shorts, longs socks with sandals, and an I LEFT MY HEART IN SAN FRANSCISCO T-shirt. A dingy blond wig covered her hair, and she had on a load of tan pancake makeup in an effort to make her look human, but I recognized her eyes. It was Claudia. "You might as well stop pretending," she said. "She knows it's you."

What was going on? Why was Wolfgang masquerading as a middle-aged spinster? And more important, why was he with Circe?

I was more confused than ever.

There was a knock at the door.

"That has to be room service this time," Wolfie said. He made a beeline for the door.

"Don't answer that," Circe and I said at the same time, but it was too late.

Before anyone could react, a woman with a birthmark pushed her way into the room and opened fire. Two men appeared behind her, carrying crosses. She shot Circe in the chest and then pointed the gun at Wolfie. The crosses forced Count Dracul and Claudia to hang back. The count ran to Circe as she fell to the floor.

I concentrated and gave a mental push. It propelled the shooter out into the hallway, where she hit the wall with a dull thud. The two men backed out of the room.

"Trinity's down!" one of them said. I concentrated again and slammed the door shut and locked it.

Ryan was already dialing 911. He stayed on the phone, but he said, "I need towels. Cover her up." He barked orders as we tried to help Circe until the paramedics arrived.

There was blood everywhere, and I noticed that Count Dracul and Claudia were restraining themselves, but there were beads of blood forming on Claudia's forehead. She looked hungry.

Wolfgang stood frozen, but when he noticed his girl-friend's distress, he finally took action and put his arm around her. "Don't look, Claudia," he said. "Think of something else."

It seemed like forever, but I finally heard the wail of sirens in the distance. They loaded Circe onto a gurney, and the count left with her.

Ryan and I sat on the couch. "I'm calling Dad," Ryan said. He took out his cell phone and dialed, and then, after a brief conversation he hung up. "Dad's on his way. He's calling your parents."

My parents. They'd be frantic by now.

Wolfie paced, and Claudia licked her lips as she stared at a spot of blood on the wall.

I felt sorry for her, but it was a crime scene. We couldn't exactly tidy up.

"Why would anyone want to shoot Circe?" I said finally.

"Who didn't want to shoot her?" Wolfgang replied.

"Come on, Wolfie. Tell me what you know."

Claudia stepped between us and took his hand. "Daisy saved your life, Wolfgang. We owe her the truth."

Wolfie cleared his throat. "Claudia and I have been going out for a while, but we knew, with all the stuff going on between the shifters and the vampires, that neither side would be happy if they found out. So we started sneaking around."

"He didn't want to," Claudia said. "But I insisted."

"Anyway, we were sitting in a tent by the beach—I set it up so Claudia could see the sun rise—and we saw them when they dumped that vampire kid. The one who almost burned up in the sun?"

"We thought that one of the Scourge saw us as they were leaving, but we weren't sure," Claudia said. "We called for help and the vampire lived."

"How did you know it was the Scourge?" Ryan asked.

"They weren't shifters, and they weren't vamps," Wolfie said. "We would have recognized them if they were."

"One of them was that woman who just shot Circe," Claudia said. "I'm sure of it."

"So why did the vampire kid say it was Weres who attacked him?" I asked.

"He had been blindfolded before he saw his attackers," Claudia explained. "But Wolfie and I saw them, so we were scared."

"I thought the kidnapped vampire said he smelled wolf," I said.

"He did," Wolfie replied, blushing. "But it was me he smelled, not his kidnappers."

"We went to my grandfather, and he told the council everything we knew," Claudia said. "They knew that the Scourge would try to eliminate us. So they called Circe."

"To help guard you?" I asked. "That's why she was holed up at the hotel?"

"Yes," she said. "Sorceresses aren't tied to the whims of the full moon and can't be repelled by a cross."

There was a knock at the door. No one moved until Chief Mendez said, "Ryan, it's me."

Liam, Nicholas, and the chief walked into the room. Mr. Bone had sent the task force. Interesting.

"Where's Grandfather?" Liam asked Claudia, but she didn't answer. She stared at the blood and then, without warning, lunged. Liam moved so quickly I didn't even see him leave the doorway, but in an instant he had grabbed Claudia by the arm and was restraining her.

She broke into loud sobs. "It's okay," he said. "It's okay." He patted her shoulder. "She isn't as old as I am," he explained to us. "She has a harder time fighting the urge."

He led her into one of the bedrooms, and after ripping off his wig, Wolfie followed.

"Daisy, are you and Ryan okay?" Nicholas asked. "Poppy and Rose are freaking out."

"We're okay," I said. "But Circe, she's definitely not okay."

"What did you tell the San Carlos police?" Chief Mendez asked.

"We didn't say anything about council business," Ryan said. "Just that three strangers came in, shot Circe, and left."

"I also didn't tell them that I'd seen the woman before," I said. "I saw her at Mr. Devereaux's condo."

"Are you sure you saw her there?" the chief said.

"Positive. She said her name was Trinity, and that was what one of the guys with her tonight called her." I paused remembering something else. "She might have had something to do with Elise Wilder's attack, too."

The chief nodded. "She does fit the description that Miss Wilder gave us."

We told them everything that happened, but I found myself falling asleep as we talked.

"Ryan, Nicholas will drive you and Daisy home," his dad

said. "Mort and I have to get Wolfgang and Claudia to a new location."

I noticed Balthazar was shivering in the corner, and I scooped him up. "I'll take Balthazar home with me," I said.

I was intrigued to see that Nicholas and Liam shook hands before everyone went their separate ways. At least my sisters' boyfriends were getting along, even if the rest of Nightshade was not.

Ryan and I didn't talk on the drive back to Nightshade, but Balthazar curled up in the back seat and snored all the way home while I kept replaying the night over and over again in my head.

CHAPTER FIFTEEN

By the next day, we got word that Circe was expected to make a full recovery. I didn't know how long she'd be in the hospital, and I knew that this might be my only chance to free Lily and Balthazar. But I would need Natalie's help.

One of my sisters had the car, so I called Sam to pick me up and take me to Slim's. When she pulled up to my house and I walked out carrying the supplies for the spell, and Balthazar, she seemed surprised.

"I hope you don't mind if he rides with us," I said.

"I just hope Sean doesn't get jealous," she said, laughing as the pig hopped into the front passenger seat.

I spotted Natalie through the window of Slim's and we rushed inside.

"Are you going to be here for a while?" I asked her breathlessly.

"I'm just hanging out," she replied.

"I found everything we need to break the spell," I said. "I'll be right back." I could hear my voice shaking with excitement.

My heart jumped. I went to Sam's car and grabbed the library books, the pen, and the dress. It had been making me nervous carrying around the very items that might save Lil from her jukebox. It might not work, but it was the only shot we had.

Natalie went into the back kitchen and then came out a few minutes later. She turned the sign to Closed and locked the front door.

"Slim's hoping we can get this over with before we completely ruin his dinner rush," Natalie said. "But I asked him to close just for a little while so we could try the spell." She was waving her hands around as she spoke.

I grinned at her. "I couldn't help but notice that enormous sparkler on your hand," I said.

She grinned back. "Yep, Slim and I are engaged."

We talked wedding details for a few minutes but then got down to business.

I handed Natalie one of the books I'd checked out of the library. "I marked the page where it talks about halting the aging process," I said. "Do you think it will work?"

She opened to the page I had indicated and read quickly. She ran a finger down the page. "I have everything I need for the antiaging spell," she said. "But I think we need one more ingredient to break the enchantment."

"What are we going to do?" I asked.

"Let me make a call," she said.

She had a brief conversation with somebody and then hung up.

"Anyone hungry?" Slim asked. "I can make some snacks. Darling, what is appropriate to serve at a de-enchantment?"

Natalie chuckled. "Nachos, I think."

Slim went into the kitchen to whip up something to eat while the rest of us waited. An elderly couple who had been finishing their meal paid their bill and left.

Finally, there was a knock at the door and Natalie answered it. I couldn't see who was on the other side of the door, but Natalie came back carrying a small jar full of a pungent liquid.

"What is that horrid smell?" Sam asked.

"The bitterness of unrequited love," Natalie said. "I need just a drop."

"Any more and it'd be a ready-made stink bomb," Sam said.

"Are you ready?" Natalie asked me.

I nodded, but my stomach did a nervous little dance, and I prayed that I wouldn't be sick.

"Positive thoughts," Natalie reminded me. "Place the dress and the pen in the circle."

I did what she asked and then stepped back. "Now what?"

"Now I do my thing," she said. "First I'll embed the spell that will preserve Balthazar and Lily at the ages they were when they were first enchanted. Then, when I'm sure it's taken, I'll try to break the original spell."

The first thing she did was head to the kitchen to forage for ingredients. She came back with strawberries and honey. She pulled a long glass bottle out of her bag and added the strawberries and honey to the liquid. She shook it vigorously, took a sip, and then said, "Perfect."

She said a couple of words and then sprinkled a bit of the liquid in the air. It dissolved immediately but left a tantalizing fragrance.

"What was that in the bottle?" I asked.

"Yearning," she said.

Then Natalie got out an old pottery bowl that was decorated with moons and stars, carefully poured a dry green powder into it, and added a drop of tears.

There was a little puff of smoke when the ingredients combined, and then nothing.

"Did it work?" Sam leaned in to get a look.

"I don't think so," Natalie said. "I don't think we have the right items."

"Don't be sorry," I said. "Thanks for trying."

"Maybe I did something wrong," Natalie said. "Or maybe there's something missing."

Sam could tell I was disappointed and gave me a hug. "We'll figure it out."

"I think I managed to conceal the antiaging spell, so if Circe ever does change her mind about releasing them, she won't know that I added a little something," Natalie said.

"I'm sure this is the pen that Circe was talking about, but

I'm not sure what item she used that belonged to Lily."

"I think it will work if you can figure out the other item," she said. She reached down and scratched Balthazar's nose. "What are you going to do with this little guy in the meantime?"

"I don't know," I admitted. "I don't really want to give him back to Circe."

"We can keep him at our place," she offered.

"What about your cat?" I asked. Natalie's familiar had never seemed that friendly to me, but cats seldom were.

"Oh, Fluffy loves company," she said.

A huge plate of nachos floated to the table, which meant my boss was back.

"Consolation nachos," Slim said.

Natalie reached over and snatched a chip. "I'm famished," she said.

"She's starving after she works her craft," Slim said.

"All magic has its price," Natalie said.

"What should we do about the pen?" I asked. "I don't think Circe knows I have it, but I don't want her to get her hands on it again."

"You can lock it in the safe in the office," Slim said.

"Do you think it will be safe there?" I asked.

"I'll make sure of it," Natalie said. "I'll add a little something so only the three of us can unlock it."

We trooped back to the office, and I put the pen in the safe.

Then Natalie dug in her bag, sprinkled a dark-colored powder over the safe, and mumbled a few words.

"That should do it," she said.

As I was getting ready to leave, Natalie handed the book back to me. "I'm going to look for a copy of this," she said. "There are some great spells in there. Where did you get it?"

"Ms. Johns, the librarian, loaned it to me. It's part of her personal collection."

"Interesting," she commented. "It's not many librarians who would loan out a rare first edition."

"What? She told me it was published in 1960," I said. I felt myself turning pale. "I had it in my backpack. Don't tell me it's valuable."

"I won't," she said. "It's priceless."

"I've got to get it back to her before the library closes," I said. I said my goodbyes and then made it to the library just in time.

"I had no idea this was such a precious book or I would never have borrowed it," I told her when I found her in her office.

"Did it help?" she asked mildly. "Did you bring it back un-damaged?"

"Yes to both questions," I said.

"Then it was a good decision," she said.

Just then, a thought occurred to me. "Do you have any

books on the history of Nightshade?" I asked. "In the general collection, I mean." I remembered someone had said something about the Weres and the vampires being at peace for over fifty years. I wondered what life in Nightshade had been like prior to that time.

"We have a nice selection of books on local history," she replied. "I'll show you." I found a couple of likely-looking items and made it to the checkout line as the five-minute warning was announced over the loudspeaker, then went home to do an hour or two of light reading about the history of my hometown. Nightshade's history was a bloody one, involving years of hatred between the shifters and the vampires. I hoped my nighttime reading wouldn't give me nightmares.

CHAPTER SIXTEEN

During the school week, I was unable to shake the feeling of dread that followed me everywhere I went. They still hadn't caught Trinity or her accomplices. Circe's shooting had made the papers, and tensions were high. They were passing it off as a random act by a crazed fan, but rumors were flying.

And the thing we feared had happened. Our senior prom was canceled. The news came during morning announcements, and there was an immediate uproar.

"I can't believe it," Penny said.

"We knew it was a possibility," I reminded her. "Everyone is freaked out about the paranormal attacks going on."

"We're the ones suffering," she said.

I raised an eyebrow. "You mean *besides* the victims?"

"You know what I mean," she said. "Everyone loses."

Penny was right. Everyone loses except the Scourge. It was their mission in life to eradicate paranormals forever. The members of the Scourge I'd met hated anyone they considered different.

Our homeroom teacher, Ms. Tapia, was still trying to restore order. For a minute it looked like everyone would ignore her, but it finally got quiet.

"Your safety is our first consideration," she reminded us.

This didn't seem to make the Nightshade High student body feel any happier.

At lunch, even Samantha was complaining. "Did you hear about prom? It's not fair."

"That blows," Sean commented.

"There isn't anything we can do about it," I said.

Ryan picked up on my bad mood and took my hand. "That gloom and doom doesn't sound like you. We'll figure something out."

"What can we do?" I refused to be cheered up.

"Penny said you mentioned an alternative prom," Samantha said.

"That was when I didn't think prom would really get canceled," I replied.

"But it's not a bad idea," Ryan said. "We could pull it off."

"We wouldn't be able to tell our parents," Samantha said. "They'd freak."

"We have to tell them. They'll notice if we get all dressed up and a limo pulls up to pick us up," I said. "We have to find a place where they think we'll be safe."

"What about Slim's?" Sam suggested. "It's right on Main Street."

"That's not a bad idea," Ryan said. "The police station is right across the street, so my dad and Officer Denton can keep an eye on things."

We decided that I would be the one to ask Slim. I wasn't sure what he'd say, but I went to the diner right after school to talk to him.

"If all the parents sign off on it, I'd gladly host an alternative prom," he said. "But it's up to you to get the parents to agree."

"Samantha can do that," I said.

He laughed. "I'm sure you're right."

The tickets went on sale three days later. Sam worked fast. She also thought of the 1950s theme, which sent the junior and senior girls of Nightshade straight to the boutiques and thrift stores for vintage prom dresses.

And right after that, I was bewailing my lack of an appropriate dress to Sam.

"Why don't you order from my designer?" she asked. Samantha had found a designer on an online craft site who did fabulous reproduction '50s dresses.

"She's ridiculously expensive," I said. "And prom's not that far away."

"I'm paying extra for a rush job," she said. "Daddy okayed the extra cost."

"I don't think I can spend that kind of money," I said. I frowned at her, but she didn't even notice. Sam had been spending her dad's money fast and furiously.

"What are you going to do? There isn't anything decent left in the stores."

She had a point. I took a bite of my so-so salad to give myself time to think.

"My grandma's closet," I finally replied. My grandmother was one of the most stylish people I knew—a trait I clearly hadn't inherited—and I'd bet money she had something I could borrow.

After school, I gave Grandma Giordano a call and explained my predicament.

"Why, I think I may have just the thing," she said. "I've been meaning to go through my closet."

Rose and Poppy decided to come with me. If clothes were involved, Poppy was there. She even let me drive.

"So, how are things going with Liam?" I asked.

"I'm not letting him bite me, if that's what you're asking."

"I'm not," I said, put off by her snarky tone. "I was just trying to make conversation. You haven't brought him around since we all had dinner."

"To be honest, you still seem skittish about the whole vampire thing," she said. "Besides, after my very public breakup with Gage . . ."

"He didn't break up with you," Rose pointed out. "The last thing he said was that he loved you."

"A breakup is a breakup," Poppy replied. She was still guarding her heart against any more pain.

"Why don't you invite him over for movie night?" I suggested. "I promise to hide all the cheesy vampire movies."

"Maybe," she said. "I'll talk to him and see what he says."

I parked the car, and we walked up the path to Grandma Giordano's. She had a bunch of planters filled with jasmine, and there was a dwarf orange tree in a pot by the entrance.

Grandma opened the door before we could even ring the bell.

"It's so good to see you girls," she said. "Come on in. Let's go straight to my closet."

Grandma's closet looked like one of those celebrity closets you saw on TV.

"This is as big as my bedroom," Poppy breathed. And she wasn't exaggerating by much.

Grandma laughed. "I converted one of the bedrooms. I just couldn't bear to let go of my memories. I even have the dress I wore to my junior prom."

"That was in the fifties, right?" I asked.

She nodded. "I think it might fit you," she said. "You're a little taller than I am, but I can let the hem out a little."

She flipped a switch and the clothes started to rotate,

carried on a circular motorized track. "The newer stuff is in the other closet," she explained.

"Grandma, you're my hero!" Poppy exclaimed.

She chuckled and then pushed the button again. "This is the fifties section," she said. She pulled out a strapless white organza dress that was patterned with tiny pink polka dots. There was a silk flower pinned to the waist.

"I wore this to a spring dance," she said. She pulled out another dress, this one white with sheer lace over the bodice and a tulle and chiffon skirt. "I wore this one to my cotillion."

"That might look good on you, Daisy," Rose said. "Try it on."

Grandma pulled out a red and black mermaid dress. "What about this one?" she said.

It looked like the dress Rizzo wore to the dance in *Grease*. I couldn't picture my Grandma wearing it. Poppy had the same thought. "You wore that, Grandma?"

"I was trying to impress a certain boy," she said. "Tall, broad shoulders, wavy dark hair. He was dreamy."

My grandfather had had wavy dark hair, at least in the pictures I'd seen of him when he was young. Grandma had a dreamy smile on her face, and her thoughts were clearly far, far away. "I miss him so much sometimes. Your father looks so much like him," she said, which confirmed that she was talking about Grandpa, who had died when I was a baby.

She stirred, then said briskly, "What about this one? It would go wonderfully with your coloring." She pulled out a tea-length dress. It was cream-colored taffeta with a navy lace overlay, sleeveless with a deep V-neck. It had a navy velvet belt and a silk flower pinned to the waist.

Grandma surveyed her closet and pulled out another armload of dresses.

"You went to a lot of dances when you were a teenager," Rose commented.

"Lucky for me," I said.

"There are matching gloves around here somewhere," Grandma Giordano said. "Ah, here they are." She handed me a long, narrow white box.

I took three of the dresses from her.

"Grandma, did you keep anything else? Something for everyday?" Poppy asked. "I want to volunteer to work the prom that night. Wouldn't it be cool if I could dress the part of a fifties waitress?"

"Daisy, why don't you try a few of the dresses on while your sisters and I look through some of the stuff in boxes?"

I stepped out of the closet with the first three gowns and laid them on the bed to get a better look.

I decided to start with the white dress. It was beautiful and fit like a dream. I went back into the closet with it on.

Poppy was wearing a red poodle skirt over her jeans, and

a pair of saddle shoes were on the floor beside her. She looked up when I came in. "No," she said, vetoing the white dress. "Too vanilla. You look like a ghost." She said the word *ghost* without a trace of melancholy, which meant, if nothing else, that Liam was easing the heartbreak of losing her first love, Gage, who was a ghost.

I marched back into the bedroom while they continued to rummage through the closet. I studied the next two choices. The daring red or the subtler navy dress?

I knew which one Poppy would choose, so I slipped on the red and black mermaid dress and slipped my feet into a pair of black heels.

"Va-voom," Grandma said when I presented myself for their inspection.

"That's the one!" Poppy crowed.

"I don't know," I said. I tugged on the plunging neckline.

"Don't wear it if you'll feel uncomfortable," Rose advised.

"Try on the navy dress next," Grandma said. "I also found these." She held out a frilly pink number and another white dress, but this one had a plainer cut and was embroidered with tiny yellow silk daisies.

The navy dress seemed to meet with Grandma's approval. "Oh, to have such a creamy complexion," she said. She tilted my chin up and looked into my eyes. "And the navy makes your eyes look even bluer, if that's possible."

"It's a little short," I said.

Grandma flipped up the hem. "Hmm. I can take the hem out about an inch," she said.

The navy was added to the maybe pile.

The pink dress made me look like I was wearing a bowl of sherbet, so I eliminated that one without even showing it to my fashion consultants.

The white dress with the yellow daisies was gorgeous. I twirled around, and the wide skirt flared as I moved.

"It's definitely the right era," Grandma said. "But it's a little too casual for prom, I think."

I was disappointed, but rallied quickly. "What about graduation? Would it work for a graduation outfit?"

"It would be perfect," Grandma said. "In fact, I wore it to my own graduation."

That left the red dress and the navy. "I can't decide!" I said.

"Why don't you take both of them home and sleep on it?" Grandma suggested. Poppy scooped up the poodle skirt, the saddle shoes, and a snowy white blouse with a Peter Pan collar. "Can I borrow these?" she asked.

"Of course," Grandma replied. "Now, who wants a snack?"

A snack at Grandma Giordano's meant espresso and cookies.

Rose looked at her watch. "Sorry, Grandma, we've got to

get going. I have tons of studying to do. But we'll see you for Daisy's birthday, right?"

"I wouldn't miss it," she assured me.

With everything going on, my impending birthday had completely slipped my mind.

CHAPTER SEVENTEEN

Saturday morning, I awoke to the sound of singing. It seemed to be coming from somewhere outside. Bleary-eyed, I stumbled over and looked out. My boyfriend was below my bedroom window, singing "Happy Birthday" off-key and at the top of his lungs.

I loved him even more when I saw that he had a cup of coffee in each hand. I opened the sash and yelled, "Give me a minute and I'll be right down."

I changed into something a little more attractive, brushed my teeth, and put my hair in a ponytail, then tiptoed down the stairs. I wasn't sure why I was tiptoeing. The rest of my family seemed to still be asleep, and if Ryan's serenade hadn't woken them up, nothing would.

Once I was outside, Ryan handed me one of the coffees and gave me a kiss. "Happy birthday."

"I didn't think I'd see you until later today," I said.

"There was no way I was going to miss another one of your

birthdays," he said. When he first found out he was a Were, he'd missed my birthday, but he'd made up for it by giving me a very special locket.

"Besides, I missed you," he added.

"You just saw me yesterday," I told him.

"I still missed you," he replied. I kissed him.

A long time later, we came up for air. I took a sip of my coffee, which had gone cold. "C'mon, let's go inside. My coffee needs to be warmed up."

When we got inside, my whole family was up. "Happy birthday," they shouted.

There were balloons at the breakfast table, and it looked like my father was in the process of whipping up enough food for twenty.

"Ryan, would you like to join us for breakfast?" Dad asked.

I smiled at him. It was nice to see Ryan and my dad getting along so well.

"I'd love to," Ryan said. "In fact, I was hoping to spend the whole day with Daisy, if that's okay?"

I waited for my dad to explode, but he smiled mildly. "Sounds like a plan."

After a leisurely breakfast, Ryan and I decided to catch an early movie.

"What time is everyone coming over?" I asked Mom.

"Four," she said. "So make sure you're back by then."

It was going to be a small celebration, just family and significant others.

When Ryan and I returned from the matinee, Poppy was setting the table in the dining room.

"It's so beautiful out," I said. "I thought we would eat outside."

"Liam's coming," she said. "So I thought we'd eat inside. If that's all right?"

I gave her a hug. "That's great. Inside is fine."

Grandma Giordano was helping in the kitchen, so I went to give her a hug.

"Where's that gorgeous boyfriend of yours?" she said in a loud, carrying voice.

"Hello, Mrs. Giordano," Ryan said. "You're looking lovely."

She was. Grandma wore a blue and white floral cardigan, a dark blue shirt, and matching trousers. She looked immaculate, even though she'd been helping my dad cook.

"How do you do that?" I asked.

"What?" she replied.

"Stay so clean when you're cooking. I always end up with sauce all over me."

She laughed. "Years of practice."

Liam and Nicholas arrived shortly after, and we all hung out in the family room until dinner was ready.

After a delicious dinner, Dad and Mom brought out this huge birthday cake. And then there were presents. Ryan gave me a pair of earrings that would look great with the locket he'd given me the year before.

"We'll clean up," Mom and Dad said.

"You two just want to canoodle in the kitchen," Grandma said.

Mom laughed. "We'll never tell."

We headed back to the family room, where everyone sprawled around in a food-induced coma.

"I'm so stuffed I can't move," Nicholas said. "And that's hard to do to a werewolf."

We all laughed, even Liam.

"There's nothing I like better than catching up with my granddaughters," Grandma said. "Now, Rose, when are you and Nicholas going to get engaged?"

Rose sputtered and blushed, but Grandma's comment made me think of Lily and Balthazar. They had just gotten engaged when their lives were changed forever by Circe. She had said something about a symbol of true love.

"That's it!" I said. "I know what Circe used to trap Lily in the jukebox."

Everyone jumped about a mile, but Rose sent me a message.

Thanks for changing the subject. There's nothing worse than being grilled by Grandma about getting married, even though she means well.

I nodded absently, my mind elsewhere. I finally stopped when Grandma gave me a strange look.

Poppy caught on. "Stop it, you two," she told us, then turned to Grandma. "They're using their powers to talk because they know we can't hear them."

"Sorry," I said. "Grandma, I need a favor. I need to get into Merriweather House. Can you help me?"

"Sounds intriguing," she said. "I'll go with you."

"Me too," Ryan said.

"I'm too tired for any detecting tonight," Poppy said.

"Sorry, Daisy," Rose said. "I'm going to pass."

I was on a roll in the detecting department.

Grandma made a quick call to one of her historical society buddies, and ten minutes later we were on our way to Merriweather House and, I hoped, a solution to Lily and Balthazar's enchantment.

"You can drive. Let me get my bag out of my trunk," she said. "Beatrice said she'd leave a key under the mat. She lives only a few blocks from the mansion."

We pulled up to the mansion and got out. Grandma carried an expensive weekender bag that was almost as big as she was, but it matched her shoes, which I knew was what really mattered. At least to Grandma.

The Merriweather House was the site of last Halloween's

Nightshade Through the Ages ball, which is when I finally found out that my beloved jukebox contained the spirit of Lily Varcol, Mrs. Wilder's sister.

Beatrice had come through. The key was right where she had said it would be.

Once inside, Grandma ran her index finger along the banister. "The caretaker is slacking off," she said. She raised her finger to show me all the dust, then reached into her bag and brought out a feather duster and cleaning supplies.

"I told Beatrice I thought the place could use a quick cleaning," she said. "And from the look of things, I'm glad I did. Now, you two, get to sleuthing while I whip this place into shape. Mrs. Wilder has been thinking about turning this old house over to the historical society, and I want it to be clean if she does."

I hugged her, and as I left her on the first floor, she was still muttering about the disgraceful state of things.

"I'll take the third floor, you take the second," I told Ryan.

"Can't we search together?" he asked. "I don't even know what we're looking for."

"You know as well as I do that we wouldn't get anything done that way," I told him. "Look for a ring. An engagement ring."

"This is so sudden," he joked.

I laughed. "Not for me," I said. "Lily's engagement ring. That's what we're looking for."

I climbed the stairs to the third floor. I assumed that was where Bam's bedroom would be.

As I walked through his room, I noticed there were several photos of Lily on his nightstand, but it was a full-length photo of the two of them that had me mesmerized. It hung opposite a huge teak four-poster bed.

In the photo, Lily wore a long white dress and some sort of flower in her hair. Bam looked debonair in a black tux and crisp white shirt. He was holding Lily's hand above his own, so that the engagement ring was proudly displayed.

A ring with a stunning ruby and a filigreed band shone on Lily's finger, but it was the happiness on their faces that glittered the brightest.

What had happened to that ring? Had it disappeared with Lily? Or was it still in the house somewhere?

I searched every square inch of the bedroom but didn't find it.

Ryan wandered in a few minutes later.

"Any luck?" he asked.

"No," I said sadly. I gestured to the photo. "But at least I know what it looks like now."

"You know, I know a thing or two about police procedure," Ryan said, "and there's a chance it was seized as evidence."

It suddenly dawned on me what Circe meant when she said that the item had been confiscated.

I needed to get ahold of whatever evidence there was in

the Nightshade police files. "Can we ask your dad to let us see the evidence from the case?"

Ryan shook his head. "I don't think so, Daisy. Only family and authorized personnel are allowed to see that kind of stuff."

That meant another late-night visit to the police station.

"Hey, Ryan," I said. "Do you still have those keys?"

He looked confused for a minute. "Keys?"

I waggled my eyebrows at him. "You know, the keys you had when we first kissed."

"Oh," he said. "I'm afraid not, but if you give me some time, I can get them."

"Fabulous," I said. "Let's go see if Grandma needs any help cleaning."

Grandma had managed to get rid of the dust and leave the rooms smelling of Lemon Pledge while we were gone. All and all, a great birthday.

But the celebrating didn't end with the weekend. Monday morning, Sam and the rest of the cheerleaders had a surprise for me. Next to the vending machines was a table piled high with cupcakes. I looked closer and noticed that every single one of them was decorated with a daisy made out of frosting.

"Happy birthday, Daisy!" Sam said. "Cupcakes for everyone."

I said to Rachel, who was in the chair next to Sam, "I can't believe you're encouraging her."

She handed me a cupcake and then shrugged. "You know Sam," she said. "She's unstoppable."

"You should have asked me to help you bake," I said. I bit into the cupcake. "Hey, these are good."

Sam gave me a little nudge. "Don't sound so surprised. I've learned a few things hanging around you."

"Yeah, how to call up Slim and get him to bake enough cupcakes for the entire high school," Jordan snorted.

"That must have been expensive," I said.

"Don't worry," Sam said airily. "Dad gave me the money."

At my frown, she added, "And your boss gave them to us for half price when he found out what they were for."

"Slim is a great boss," I said. Despite myself, I grinned.

I took a bite of my cupcake and then headed for my first class. Turning eighteen was turning out to be sweeter than I expected.

CHAPTER EIGHTEEN

Two weeks later, most kids were going to their prom. Instead, Nightshade teens got all dressed up and went to the alternative prom.

When Ryan and I walked in to the diner, the first thing I noticed was a huge banner that read NOT THE PROM in bold letters.

Slim's was stuffed with high school students decked out in 1950s chic.

Flo was working the fryer, but I caught a glimpse of her when she brought out a huge chafing dish full of the delicious potatoes. Her only nod to the theme was that she had her jeans rolled up and wore bobby socks and saddle shoes. She had on one of her many T-shirts. This one read FRIES BEFORE GUYS, which made me laugh. We waved to each other before she headed back to the kitchen.

Poppy and Liam were working the soda fountain. Liam wore a white button-down with the sleeves rolled up, a bow tie, and bore a slight resemblance to Tobey Maguire's character in *Pleasantville*. Poppy wore Grandma's red poodle skirt and shirt and had braided her hair into perky pigtails and threaded red and white ribbon through the braids.

I spotted Natalie, who was wearing a bright pink uniform and white roller skates decorated with pink pompoms. Her engagement ring gleamed as she skated by with a tray of food.

"I didn't know you could roller-skate," I told her when she stopped to say hi.

She examined the vintage four-wheelers ruefully. "I can in-line fine," she said. "But I just can't get the hang of four-wheelers. Slim told me to just use my inlines, but I wanted to look like an authentic fifties carhop. So I did a little spell, and now the skates do all the work."

The menu was simple. Cheeseburgers and fries, shakes or vanilla colas. Slim had made allowances for the unique tastes of Nightshade residents and included extra-extra-rare burgers and some unusual choices for shake flavors.

Ryan wore a gray flannel suit, white shirt, and thin red tie, while Sean channeled his inner early Elvis with a shiny gold wide-lapeled suit, black shirt, and pants. Some of the guys opted for the beatnik look and wore black jeans with turtleneck sweaters, while others went the simple route with rolled-up jeans, white T-shirts, and black leather jackets.

The girls, on the other hand, went all out. Jordan wore a lavender number with an iridescent poufy skirt and a little peplumed lace jacket. Rachel wore a dark green long dress that fit her like a glove. Her date couldn't stop staring at her.

But it was Samantha's butterscotch floor-length sarong that was stunning. Her upswept hairdo showed off a pair of huge diamond earrings.

"You look like Grace Kelly," I said.

"Who is that?" she asked.

"Was in a lot of Hitchcock films, married a prince," I summarized.

"So, you're saying I look like a princess? Thank you," she said. "Daddy's been treating me like one lately." She touched the earrings self-consciously. "He gave them to me today. You look fabulous too. Very prom queen," she said.

I'd finally decided to go with the daring red and black dress but had asked Rose to sew a black lace panel into the plunging neckline, since I wasn't crazy about revealing half my cleavage.

"I can't be the prom queen, because this is not the prom," I said. I pointed to the banner smugly.

She smiled serenely. "Of course you can't be queen of the prom," she replied. Her apparent acquiescence didn't reassure me.

"Everything turned out so well," I said. "I can't believe how fast you got everything organized, Sam."

She shrugged off the compliment. "It's easy to boss people

around." She leaned in and said, "I heard Wolfgang is going to be here tonight."

"He's only a freshman," I said. "And he's part of the reason prom got canceled. I thought he would be on lockdown after Circe's shooting."

"I heard he's coming too," Ryan said. "I think he's going with Christy Hannigan."

"I didn't even know they were dating," I said. "What about Claudia?"

Ryan changed the subject. "Are you hungry?"

"Starving," I admitted. We got our food and sat down at a table with Samantha and Sean and a bunch of cheerleaders and their dates.

Mom and Dad had thankfully opted to stay home for the evening, but I spotted Rose and Nicholas holding hands by the jukebox. Some chaperones they were. They were staring into each other's eyes, oblivious to everything going on around them. I recognized the dress she wore as another one of Grandma's. This one was a day dress, a black and white toile, which she paired with simple black flats. She'd tied up her hair with a thick red ribbon.

Lil was cooperating this evening and cranked out a steady playlist of songs from the 1950s. "Sea of Love" was playing when I walked up, but she changed it to "You're So Fine" by the Falcons.

"Thanks," I said. "I haven't forgotten about you, Lily."

On the way back to the table I bumped into Lilah Porter, who wore a cream and black fitted sheath and mile-high heels. When I looked closer, I saw the cream material was printed with tiny mermaids. She had a rope of pearls draped around her neck that I swore looked real.

"I like your dress," I told her with a grin. "And your necklace."

She grinned back. "The pearls are a family heirloom," she said. "One of my ancestors, er, found them one night during a swim."

Coming from a mermaid family did have its perks.

Penny and Tyler came in late. Penny looked as pretty as I'd ever seen her in a coral chiffon dress with a sheer material draped over the bodice and bows at the shoulders. There were also bows scattered throughout the skirt.

After we ate, we migrated out back to the parking lot in the rear of the restaurant. There wasn't enough room in the restaurant for a dance floor, so one had been set up in one of those huge white tents people rented for weddings.

Flo's boyfriend, Vinnie, had pulled some strings, so not only were Side Effects May Vary playing, but a trio called Howling Monkeys was also performing. Howling Monkeys consisted of two brothers who looked nothing alike, as well as their little sister Casey, who was around twelve but sang like she'd experienced years of heartbreak.

"I love this song!" I said, grabbing Ryan and heading for the dance floor. Several songs later, the music abruptly ended and I looked up to see Sam standing in front of the microphone.

"May I have your attention, please?" she said. She waited for it to get quiet and then said, "Although our real prom was canceled, which was a bummer, I want to thank Slim and Natalie for hosting this event and all the people who volunteered for the Not the Prom."

We all broke into loud applause, and there were several wolf whistles from the crowd.

She waited for the applause to stop and then said, "And now it's time to crown the king and queen of the Not the Prom," she said. "But first I'd like to present the members of the royal Not the Prom court. Please join me if you hear your name called. Penny Edwards and Tyler Diaz."

Penny squealed with excitement, and everyone laughed. She ran to the bandstand, and Tyler, even with his long legs, had a hard time keeping up with her.

"Rachel King and Brian Miller," she continued. "Jordan Kelley and Reese Calhoun. Samantha Devereaux and Sean Walsh," she said.

"That's me," she added, in case anyone at Nightshade High didn't already know.

She paused while the crowd applauded. She waited until everyone had joined her at the bandstand, then reached behind the drum set and handed something to Sean. When she and Sean went back to the line, they were carrying daisy chains in their arms.

"I have a bad feeling about this," I said to Ryan, who just grinned at me.

"The king and queen of Not the Prom are"—she paused dramatically—"Ryan Mendez and Daisy Giordano."

Ryan grabbed my hand and we walked up to Sam. "I thought we agreed that since there wasn't a prom, there shouldn't be a queen," I told her quietly, but I smiled when I said it. It was a nice thing for Sam to do, and if I was truthful, part of me was thrilled to be a queen, even if it was for a pseudo prom.

She gave me a dazzling smile and put the daisy chain around Ryan's neck. She nodded at Sean, who put the daisy chain he had around my neck.

Then Sam said, "I present your king and queen, Ryan Mendez and Daisy Giordano."

Ryan and I joined hands and took a bow.

Ryan and I were slow dancing when Wolfgang walked in with his date. Obviously, he didn't get the memo about the theme, because he wore khakis, a striped shirt, and a loud tie. Christy followed behind him with Claudia and her date, a Nightshade junior named Henry.

Christy wore a hot pink dress, but the other girl's pale skin and blood red gown were what drew everyone's eyes.

Surprisingly—or maybe unsurprisingly, since it was Wolfgang—he all but ignored Christy and pulled Claudia onto the dance floor, where they proceeded to make out. Christy looked unconcerned and stood chatting at one end of the tent with Claudia's date.

Right after Wolfgang arrived, Chief Mendez, Officer Denton, and Mr. Bone slipped in and tried to look like they were mingling, but I noticed how often their eyes darted around, scanning the crowd for . . . what?

"What's going on?" I asked Ryan.

"W-what do you mean?"

"I mean, why is your dad here? And don't tell me to chaperone either. Out with it."

He looked guilty. "I can't tell you right now," he said over the music.

Something was definitely up. I sighed. "I like a mystery more than the next person, but why can't we just have a normal prom just once?"

The song ended and the band announced a fifteen-minute break. I dragged Ryan into a quiet corner and grilled him for information.

"Now tell me the truth," I said.

"Wolfgang and Claudia," he started to say, but I interrupted him.

"Why are they here now with other people?" I asked. Then

I answered my own question. "It's a trap, isn't it?"

He nodded again. "You can't say anything," he said. "Not even to Sam."

"I won't," I told him.

Sam and Sean joined us. "What are you two talking about so secretively?" she said. "Spill."

I looked at Ryan. "Just after-prom plans," I said.

"Ooh, anything interesting?" Sam asked, wiggling her eyebrows suggestively.

I knew what she was really asking.

"We refuse to be a prom-night cliché," I said, trying not to blush. "Besides, we all promised to be on our best behavior. No sneaking off. So it's movies at my house. Science-fiction marathon. Want to join us?"

Our conversation was cut short by the sound of shrieking coming from somewhere outside the tent.

Poppy and Liam walked in, and they each had a tight grip on the arm of a still-shrieking woman.

Her hair had been dyed a frightful shade of burgundy, but I recognized her. It was the woman who'd masqueraded as my postal carrier, the woman who'd knocked on the Devereaux door when I spent the night—the woman who had shot Circe.

"We caught her trying to put poison in the shake machine," Liam said. And that's when I realized the woman hadn't dyed her hair. A sticky dark red shake was dripping down her head, but I could still see her birthmark.

Poppy grinned. "I gave her some of my special telekinesis whammy," she said, "and a Bloodbath shake ended up all over her."

I tried not to think about the ingredients in that particular dessert, but I suddenly understood why Liam had volunteered for shake duty.

"It was all I could do not to bite her," Liam said. "Especially when she tried to go after Poppy." He wrapped his arms around my sister. The blissful look on both their faces convinced me they were in love.

The chief read the woman her rights as he snapped a pair of handcuffs on her and hauled her off to jail.

"This isn't over," the woman shouted. "Not by a long shot."

The chief ignored her but did stop to shake hands with Mr. Bone, who seemed absolutely delighted with the turn of events.

I stalked up to him. "I hope it was worth it," I said.

"Daisy, you seem perturbed," he replied. "Aren't you pleased? We believe that woman we just arrested was the leader of the Scourge."

"Are you sure?" I said.

"We have just captured the person who was responsible for your father's abduction," he said. "And your father is headed to the station now to identify her."

"I hope it was worth Circe getting shot," I explained. "I don't particularly like Circe Silvertongue, but I didn't want her to get hurt."

"She was aware of the dangers," he said mildly.

"How is she doing, anyway?" I asked.

"Recuperating," he said. "She has a remarkable ability to heal."

Probably a spell. I wondered why she hadn't made herself invincible, but then I remembered Natalie's comment that all magic had a price. Maybe Circe hadn't wanted to pay the price.

"So, you're just letting Circe off the hook about Balthazar and Lily?"

"She's not off the hook," he said. "We're working on it."

"Do you honestly think she's going to stick around after her usefulness has ended?"

"Circe isn't going anywhere," Mr. Bone said. He changed the subject. "I didn't get the chance to tell you how grateful the council is to you for your quick actions the night she was shot."

"Ryan's the one who called 911," I pointed out.

"Yes, Ryan too, of course," he replied. He gestured to where Ryan was standing. "Now, why don't you join your young man and enjoy the rest of the dance?"

I decided to take his advice. There was nothing more I could do tonight, and my father's kidnapper had been captured. I could finally relax.

CHAPTER NINETEEN

Ryan came up to me after Mr. Bone had left.

"What was that all about?" he asked.

"Mr. Bone is convinced they've captured the leader of the Scourge," I explained.

"That's great news," he said. "Now let's enjoy the rest of the night. We need to have memories to hold on to when we're apart."

"You're right," I said. "C'mon, let's dance."

After all the excitement, it was nice to go back to pretending that a dance in Nightshade could be normal. As Ryan whirled me around, I vowed to let go of my cares and just enjoy the moment.

We danced until almost everyone else had left. It was very late, but I didn't want to budge from where I was.

Ryan brushed a stray curl out of my eyes and said, "I could stay like this all night."

I didn't notice when Slim came into the tent, but he cleared his throat and said, "It's closing time, kids."

I looked up at Ryan and gave him a wry grin. "Apparently we're overstayed our welcome."

Ryan and I pulled apart reluctantly and went to find Sean and Sam. They weren't in the tent, but we eventually found them in a booth in the restaurant, splitting a sundae.

"Are you guys ready to head to my house?" I asked them.

"We'll be right behind you," Sam said.

As Ryan and I headed for the door, Lil started a new song, "Mistaken Identity" by Kim Carnes. I ignored it at first, but then she followed that quickly with "Wrong" by Depeche Mode and then "The One That Got Away" by Bon Jovi. Lil was definitely trying to tell me something.

I turned to Ryan. "I think Lil's trying to tell me that someone else is still out there."

She repeated the songs while we stood and listened.

Finally, Ryan said, "Are you thinking what I'm thinking?"

"That there's still another member of the Scourge on the loose? Yes."

"Not only that," he said slowly. "But it sounds like Lil doesn't think Trinity is the leader."

"Then who is?" I replied. The whole way home, I pondered Lil's clues.

My parents were in the family room. There was a bowl of popcorn between them and a movie in the DVD player. They were waiting up for us and pretending not to.

Dad yawned and stretched unconvincingly. "How was the dance?" he asked.

"It was fun," I said. I hesitated. "Except—"

Mom cut me off. "Ryan's dad called us and told us what happened."

"I've already been to the precinct to identify her," Dad reassured me. "I recognized her voice."

"So she was the one who drugged you?" I asked.

He faltered for a minute. "I still don't remember that part," he said.

Ryan and I exchanged glances. I shook my head. I didn't want to tell my dad about the jukebox's clue until I'd had time to process Lil's message. Besides, Dad looked like the weight of the world had been lifted from his shoulders.

Dad could barely restrain his glee. "They're finally out of my life for good."

"That's great, Dad," I said.

"Now I think it's time for bed," Mom said.

I remembered something. "I invited Sean and Samantha to watch movies with us. It's okay, right?"

Mom nodded. "I always sleep better when I know you're in the house. Why don't you see if Samantha wants to sleep over?"

"There's not much of the night left," I pointed out. "A bunch of us are supposed to meet at the Donut Hole for breakfast at six a.m."

"Well, see if she wants to stay over anyway," Dad said. "Spenser is out of town."

"He is?" I was surprised. I was certain Sam said he'd given her the earrings *today*.

"He's been gone for over a week. Book tour stuff," he replied. "Can you believe it?"

I couldn't. Mr. Devereaux wasn't telling the truth about the book tour. If Sam had seen him today, he must be in town, but he wasn't going to work for some reason.

My dad gave me an odd look, and I realized I'd been lost in thought. He was still waiting for a reply.

I shrugged. "Sam didn't mention it."

My parents said good night. Ryan and I settled in on the couch and were enjoyably engaged when the doorbell rang.

"I'll get it," Ryan said. He came back with Sean and Sam.

"You haven't put the movie in yet," Sam said.

Ryan blushed revealingly. "We were waiting for you."

"Is that what they're calling it these days?" Sean said.

"What do you guys want to watch first?" I asked. "We have *Alien*, all the *Terminators*, and old-school *Planet of the Apes*."

I fell asleep halfway through *Terminator 2*, and when I woke up I was wrapped in Ryan's arms, on the couch. He was dreaming—I could tell by the way his eyelids twitched. I glanced over at the other couch. Sam and Sean were asleep, scrunched up in the love seat.

I stayed as still as I could and relished the feeling of being held safe in my boyfriend's arms, until Sean let out a loud snore and shattered the moment.

Out the window, I could see the first pink rays of dawn. I tried to go back to sleep, but the puzzles dancing around in my brain wouldn't let me. I finally gave up and carefully slid out of Ryan's arms and tiptoed to the kitchen to make coffee.

The smell of brewing coffee must have woken everyone up, because one by one they staggered into the kitchen.

I handed Ryan a cup and then the sugar bowl. He had a sweet tooth, but not in an eat-every-donut-in-sight doppel-ganger sort of way.

"Do you feel like heading for the breakfast thing?" I asked.

"Why not?" he replied.

"I'm always up for donuts," Sean said.

"I'm a mess," Sam said. "I need to go home and shower first."

"Take one here," I suggested.

While Ryan and Sean went next door to clean up at Sean's house, Sam and I freshened up. After her shower, Sam dug into her tote bag for a change of clothes.

More new clothes, I noticed. Even the bag was new. She got dressed and then slipped on a thick gold bracelet.

"Is that from Sean?" I asked.

"Daddy brings me back something from every trip," she

said. "And he's been gone a lot lately. But I don't mind a few guilt presents." For a minute she sounded like the old Sam, my nemesis and total stuck-up cheerleader.

"So, everything's going well . . . financially?"

She shrugged. "I guess so. Daddy never tells me anything. Now, get in the shower or we'll be late and all the good donuts will be gone." That was definitely the Sam I knew and loved. Snarky Sam would never have eaten a donut, let alone admitted that she was looking forward to it.

Some of our classmates were already there. We waved to Jordan and Rachel and their dates through the window. They'd put a bunch of little tables together to form one enormous table.

Ryan and Sean went to place our order while Sam and I joined the group.

I sat next to Lilah. She wore spanking-new UC Santa Barbara sweats, and her hair was still wet, probably from an early-morning dip in the ocean.

"Nice sweats," I said. "Is that where you're going?"

"Yup," she said. "They have a great art program, and it's practically on the beach."

"Are you going to sing?" I asked without thinking.

Brian Miller looked up at our conversation. "Sing?" he said incredulously. "Lilah?"

Lilah gave me a little wink that no one else caught. "Daisy, everyone knows I can't sing a note."

Not unless she's in mermaid form, that is, I thought. She had a voice meant to lure sailors to the sea. If Brian ever heard her real voice, he wouldn't know what hit him.

My question started an avalanche of conversation about college plans. Everyone chattered away about it while I sat in silent misery. I was the unwanted one, going nowhere, doing nothing.

"What about you, Daisy?" Rachel asked.

The question was well-intentioned, but it brought a lump to my throat. I could practically see a neon LOSER sign flash above my head. I pushed away my donut and mumbled something about a culinary-arts class, which, compared to their plans, sounded about as glamorous as being a professional file clerk.

It was the sympathetic looks that really got to me. Obviously, everyone had already heard that I hadn't even gotten a reply from a single college. I got up from the table. "I need to check my work schedule," I said in a tiny voice, then fled the donut shop without looking back.

I took refuge at Slim's, which was right across the street from the Donut Hole. I sat at the counter, and Flo took one look at me and made me a giant vanilla latte topped with a mountain of whipped cream.

"What's the problem, Daisy?" she asked.

"I'm a loser," I said. I took a sip of my coffee and nearly burned my tongue. "See? I can't even drink coffee properly."

"Why do you think you're a loser?" she asked.

"Because I'm going nowhere. Everyone else is leaving for college and I'm stuck here."

"I know how you feel," she replied.

"You do?" The surprise was apparent in my voice.

She raised an eyebrow. "Did you think I always wanted to be a waitress at a diner?" she said wryly.

"I guess not," I said. Truth be told, I hadn't thought about it much at all. Before now.

"What happened?"

"Our parents died and I felt compelled to stay in Nightshade with my brother," she said. "It was the right thing to do, and I don't regret it. Sometimes you have to make the hard choice, Daisy. But make sure you're the one doing the choosing."

"Thanks for the coffee, Flo," I said. "And the talk."

Ryan met me on my way back to the donut shop. "Are you okay?"

"Fine," I lied. "I just needed to check the schedule, that's all."

He picked up on the fact that I didn't want to talk about it and dropped the subject.

"Jordan's having a party next Saturday night. Want to go?"

"What kind of a party?" I said suspiciously.

"No big deal," he said, a bit too casually. "Just an 'I got into Dartmouth' party."

"I have to work," I said. I had no idea of my schedule, since

I had forgotten to look, but I'd volunteer for that shift if I had to. "But you go ahead without me."

"I don't want to go without you," Ryan said, but he didn't sound completely sincere. Who could blame him? It was senior year, and I knew he wanted to experience everything it had to offer.

"Go," I said. "Maybe I can meet you after work."

He took me home, and I collapsed into bed and slept until the sun went down.

At school on Monday, I was still groggy from lack of sleep and had a steaming mug of coffee from home. I sat at one of the tables outside and stared at a wall.

Ryan's voice calling my name finally brought me out of my fog.

"Daisy, I've been calling you and calling you," he said. "You were really zoned out."

"Just tired, I guess," I told him.

"I think I have a solution to your college issue," he said. "Why haven't you called to find out what's going on with your applications?"

"Honestly, I haven't had much time," I replied, but a tiny spark of excitement flared at his suggestion.

He gave me a skeptical look.

"Okay, I'm afraid," I admitted. "What if no one wants me?"

"I want you," he said. "Always."

I leaned in and kissed him.

"You're right," I said. "I'm going to give the UC Nightshade Admissions Office a call. It's almost eight. Someone should be there." I grabbed my cell and dialed.

The woman at the other end was courteous but ultimately couldn't help me. "I'm so sorry," she said. "I can't pull up your record right now."

I just couldn't get a break. "Why not?"

She lowered her voice. "I'm not supposed to say."

"I'm desperate," I told her. "I haven't even gotten a letter, and I've been waiting forever."

"I don't know that the information will be of any help," she said.

"Please," I begged her.

"Our computers were hacked into," she said. "Information was compromised on thousands of students, including those applying for the fall. It's a mess." Then, in a louder voice, she said, "Our systems should be up and running again in a few days. Please call back then. Have a good day."

Then she hung up. I hoped she wouldn't get into any trouble.

"At least I tried," I said. "But why would anyone want to hack into a university database?"

Ryan thought for a minute. "I would guess that at least fifty percent of the students at UC Nightshade are paranormals. Do you think the Scourge could be behind it?"

"I don't know what to think," I said. "But it's worth letting Nicholas know. He can tell the rest of the council."

I was boycotting council meetings. They probably didn't even notice, but I was still peeved that they'd let Circe off while Lily still languished in the jukebox and Balthazar remained in a pig.

CHAPTER TWENTY

It turned out that I really did have to work the Saturday night of Jordan's party, which eased my conscience a bit. My mood improved at the thought that it was a huge computer error and not some personal flaw that accounted for my lack of acceptance at UC Nightshade.

Still, it didn't change the fact that I didn't know what my plans were for the fall.

I did know, however, that I was becoming this whiny self-obsessed person, and I didn't like her very much. I vowed to shape up and quickly.

Which is why I didn't say no when Sam approached me about the senior talent show. The talent show was a tradition, and the date of the performance was always announced a mere forty-eight hours before the actual event.

Everyone in the senior class was supposed to participate, but the rules were that you couldn't do something you were really talented at doing. So Sam couldn't boss people around, and I couldn't bake a cake. And we weren't allowed to practice more than once before the show. People broke a few of the rules sometimes, but the idea was to be as spontaneous as possible.

"Want to do something together?" she said.

"Wouldn't you rather perform with Sean?" I asked.

"He's doing an act with Ryan. Very hush-hush," she said.

I remembered my vow to try to get into the spirit of things.

"What do you have in mind?"

"Can you sing or dance?" Samantha said.

"No," I said.

"Perfect," she said. "Then that's what we're going to do."

I smothered a groan.

"You already said yes," Sam reminded me. "Besides, all those years of gymnastics have to be good for something."

After a couple of hours of debate, we finally agreed on a song, "I Love Rock and Roll," which was definitely done better by Joan Jett and the Blackhearts.

"Do you have any leather pants?" Sam asked me.

"No," I said. "And I don't intend to buy any." Sam had the body for tight leather pants. I did not.

"Do you think Nurse Phillips would let you borrow a pair of hers?" she said.

I sent her a horrified look. "Poppy has a leather jacket I can borrow," I said. "I am not, under any circumstances, appearing in front of my classmates in leather pants."

Forty-eight hours later, we were backstage at the talent show. Sam had chosen to go the full black-leather route. She wore skintight black leather pants and a short leather jacket over a red shirt.

I did my best tough-girl impression in cheetah-print leggings and a black T-shirt. My hair was curling wildly about my face. Poppy had teased it until it added about six inches to my already-tall frame.

The faculty advisor put a bunch of numbers into the hat to decide what order we would perform in.

Sam reached in and pulled out a number while I prayed we wouldn't have to go first.

"Seventh," she said. "That's lucky, right?"

I started stretching, my body protesting as I used muscles that I hadn't even thought about since I quit the cheerleading team.

Penny and Tyler were the first to go on, but judging from their laughter, it didn't seem to bother them. Penny was dressed as Sandy in *Grease*, after the big makeover, and Tyler was wearing something very similar to what he wore to prom—black jeans and a black T-shirt. They were obviously going to sing "You're the One That I Want." We heard the music start and then Tyler and Penny began to sing. I was right about their song choice. Penny was a little pitchy at first, but she ended strong. They finished to a burst of applause.

Then a couple of the football players threw lit batons in the air and caught them.

"That's cheating a little," Ryan said. "Brian Miller's sister is a twirler for marching band."

The next performers were Jordan and Rachel, who did a comedy routine that had the crowd in stitches.

"Don't look so nervous," Ryan said. "This is supposed to be fun."

He and Sean were wearing matching white shirts with black vests and black pants.

"What are you doing for the performance?" I asked.

He only smiled and said, "You'll see."

I bit my nails while I was waiting for our number to be called. There was a time when I was used to performing in public. As a gymnast.

Then it was Samantha's and my turn. I put on Poppy's black leather jacket, took a deep breath, and followed Sam as she strutted onto the stage.

When the music started, I took a deep breath and waited for my cue. The good thing about the song we'd chosen was that it needed to be belted out, so I really used my lungs as I sang.

The crowd started to sing along, and suddenly, I felt freer than I'd felt in months. While Sam sang the last few notes, I launched myself across the stage and went into a handstand and then down into a split as the song ended.

The crowd shouted its approval, and Sam and I took a

brief bow, then ran offstage, sweaty and exhilarated.

"That was fun," I said. "I'm so glad you talked me into it."

She linked arms with me. "Let's slip into the audience so we can watch the guys."

We found seats at the end of a row near the front.

I noticed quite a few strangers in the audience, which was a little unusual. The talent show was open to the public, but I couldn't imagine wanting to sit through it unless you either were a graduating senior or knew and loved one.

There was a woman sitting next to Mr. Devereaux. They seemed to know each other quite well and whispered to each other during the performances. She wore a white trench coat, scarf, and huge sunglasses that made her look a little bit like a bug.

I nudged Samantha. "Is that your father's new girlfriend?"

"I don't know who that is," she said, dismissing the woman with a glance. "But Daddy dates a lot of women."

We sat through three other acts before Ryan and Sean came onstage. Reese and Andres joined them, and the four broke into a song I'd never heard of called "Girl of My Dreams." I was happy to see that the animosity between them seemed to have disappeared.

"I would never have guessed a barbershop quartet," I said.

"I didn't even know Sean could sing," Samantha admitted.

After that, we sat in silence, mesmerized by their voices. Halfway through, all four boys left the stage and walked down the aisles, singing as they went. They were obviously searching for specific people. Sean and Ryan stopped in front of Sam and me. Ryan took my hand and knelt in front of me just as the last bars of the song faded away.

I looked around and saw that the other three boys had done the same thing. Sean was next to us, kneeling in front of Sam. Andres was kissing Lilah's hand, and Reese had Jordan in a low dip.

The crowd jumped to their feet and gave the guys a standing ovation.

CHAPTER TWENTY-ONE

It was the end of May, and the feeling at Nightshade High was one of high excitement, mixed with a tinge of melancholy. Everyone seemed hyperaware that this was a time of lasts. It was certainly affecting me that way. Every time I walked down the hall, I knew it would be one of the last few times I went to my locker or ate lunch with Ryan and my friends in the cafeteria, that these were my last days of being a high school student.

Even Sam's ordering me around took on a certain bittersweet quality.

There was less than a month before I was going to graduate from Nightshade High, but I wasn't really looking forward to it. The conversation at the donut shop kept ringing in my ears. Was I destined for college at all?

One Monday afternoon I was moping on the couch in old sweats and hadn't bothered with a shower. Poppy came in and turned the television channel without asking, which was something that normally only mildly annoyed me. Today I decided to pick a fight with her.

"Hey, I was watching that," I said. "Could you stop being so self-absorbed for just ten seconds and ask before you change the channel?"

Poppy practically dropped the remote, she was so surprised.

"Sorry," she said shortly. She didn't seem like she meant it though.

"What's your problem?" I snarled at her.

"You're completely unbearable these days," Poppy said. "What's the matter with you?"

"I'm such a loser," I said.

"What are you talking about?" She moved my legs out of the way and sat next to me.

"Everyone says long-distance relationships never work," I said. "And you should hear everyone else's college plans. Ryan should be going out with someone like Jordan or Rachel instead of a loser like me."

"What's this really about?" she asked me shrewdly. "The Daisy I know would rather claw out her own eyes than give up Ryan Mendez, so what's the story?"

"I still haven't gotten any acceptance letters," I wailed, bursting into tears. "Not even from UC Nightshade."

"That's not right," she said with gratifying speed. "There's something rotten in the state of Nightshade."

"I called admissions, and they said their database was down."

"When was that?"

"I don't know," I said. "A couple of weeks ago."

"Why don't you call them again?"

I followed my sister's advice, but the phone call wasn't that illuminating. "Yes, there was an issue with our database, but it's been resolved. New letters have been mailed out," the woman on the phone said.

"You can't tell me if I've been accepted or not?" I asked.

"I'm afraid not. You should receive your replacement letter any day."

I thanked her and hung up the phone.

"Well?" Poppy asked.

"I have to wait until I get the new letter," I said.

"That sucks," she replied.

No kidding.

But by Friday my mood had improved.

"Guess what I finally got my hands on?" Ryan said. He jingled a set of keys in front of my face.

"Excellent," I said. "When can we do it?"

"How about tonight?" he said. "It's Memorial Day weekend and Officer Denton and Dad are always busy with the tourists."

Ryan was right. There was no sign of Chief Mendez or Officer Denton when we slipped into the precinct. I had remembered my handy-dandy penlight and shone it around so that we wouldn't break a toe or anything.

"The old files are in storage," he whispered.

We passed by the morgue, and Ryan swept me into his arms for a quick kiss. "Just for old times' sake," he said.

"As enjoyable as that was," I said, "we're on a tight schedule."

The old files were stored in a creepy basement room with bad lighting and a musty smell. Row upon row of metal shelving contained white storage boxes with a year and a name written in a black Sharpie on the front.

"Exactly how old is Mrs. Wilder?" Ryan asked. "That might help us figure out what year it's filed under."

"I don't know," I said. "Maybe she's in her eighties? Lily was her older sister. Mrs. Wilder was a little girl when Lily disappeared."

It felt like we'd already been there a long time, and I was worried we'd get caught and Ryan would get into trouble.

"Maybe the evidence file was misfiled," I suggested.

Ryan looked offended.

"I don't mean by your dad," I added. "How far back have you looked?"

"Nineteen thirties," he said.

"Is there anything earlier? It's got to be here." Just as I said it I spotted the name VARCOL on one of the boxes on the top shelf. "This is it."

Ryan grabbed it and put it on the floor. We sat and looked through it. I read quickly. "It shows the ring was entered into evidence, but it's not here," I said.

Ryan lifted up the box. "There's a hole in the bottom. Maybe it fell out."

With an inward shudder, I lay on the floor and shone the penlight under the shelving. I caught a gleam when the light hit an object.

"I see something," I said. I stretched my arm out and wiggled closer in order to reach it.

I closed my hand over a small, cold object and brought it out from under the shelving. Lily Varcol's engagement ring was in the palm of my hand. I felt like shouting with joy but didn't want anyone to hear us.

Could it be so simple? Could it have been in the old police files all this time?

I couldn't wait until the morning, when I could call Natalie. I was scheduled to work anyway. I'd see her even before Slim's opened.

"We'd better get out of here," Ryan said.

I put the ring in my pocket, and we managed to sneak out without getting caught.

Ryan parked in front of my house and turned off the engine.

"Ryan, I can't tell you how much this means to me. Thanks so much for going with me tonight."

"You know I'd do anything for you. You have a smudge on your face," he said. Right before he kissed me.

I was a bundle of nerves, though, and couldn't enjoy the moment. "I'm taking the ring to work tomorrow," I said. "I'll give it to Lily as soon as we break the enchantment."

After we said good night, I went up to my room, still too keyed up to sleep. What should I do with the ring? I finally decided to put it on a gold chain and conceal it under my clothing.

But when I got to work the next morning, there was an unfamiliar face behind the grill.

"Where's Slim?" I asked Flo.

She was wearing a skirt and a T-shirt with cut-off sleeves. Today's tee read PLEASE DON'T FEED THE DEMONS.

"He and Natalie are taking a little vacation," she said. "Manfred's cooking while Slim's gone."

"When will they be back?"

The disappointment I felt must have shown, but Flo misunderstood the reason. "Don't worry, they'll be back before your commencement ceremony. And I'm watching Balthazar."

She pointed in the direction of the jukebox. There he was, curled up against Lil.

I was beyond disappointed. Graduation was two weeks away, and there's no way I'd be able to break the enchantment without Natalie. Lily and Bam had waited this long. It looked like they'd have to wait a little while longer.

CHAPTER TWENTY-TWO

The next couple of weeks were filled with senior finals, awards night, and picking up my cap and gown before the commencement ceremony. Finally, it was the day before graduation and I was kind of at loose ends for a change. Mom shooed me out of the house.

"Go on," she said. "Your father and I want to cook the food for your graduation dinner."

"I can help," I said. "Besides, Mom, I already told you that we could just go out to eat."

"I'd rather cook here," she said. "Every restaurant in town will be packed with graduation parties."

I couldn't convince her, so instead I reached over and snatched an apple slice.

Mom smacked my hand. "That's for the pie. Why don't you go find that cute boyfriend of yours?"

"You're sure I can't help with anything?" I asked.

"Go ahead," Mom said. "Have some fun with your friends and Ryan before everyone leaves for college."

Sam was babysitting Katie, and Sean and Ryan were off on some guy bonding thing. I drifted into Slim's and took a seat at the counter next to Flo. Today's tee read THE FOUR PRETTY PONIES OF THE APOCALYPSE. So much for a kinder, gentler Flo.

"Present from Vinnie?" I asked. I gestured to her shirt.

She grinned. "Nope," she said. "I bought it. One for me and one for him."

"I like it," I replied.

"No plans for today?" she asked.

"Not really," I said. "I feel kind of in limbo."

"I have something that will cheer you up," she said. She hopped down off the stool. "I'll be right back."

While I waited for Flo to come back, I went to say hi to Lil. I fished for some change and deposited it into the machine.

"I've had a lot going on lately, Lil," I said. "But I haven't forgotten you. We found your engagement ring! Hopefully now the spell will work."

Her response was to play "We Gotta Get Out of This Place" by the Animals.

"I promise," I said. "Besides, I'm staying right here in Nightshade. Even if Circe won't cooperate, I'll find a way to free you. Balthazar too."

Flo came back holding an envelope, which she presented to me with a flourish. "It's from Slim and me. Your graduation present."

"You didn't have to!" I said. "Thank you."

The melancholy strains of Chris Isaak's "Graduation Day" floated through the air.

"We wanted to," she said. "And besides, you don't even know what it is. So open it already."

I ran my finger along the flap and opened the envelope. Inside was a handmade card and a check. The amount made my eyes bug.

"Flo, I can't take this," I said. "It's too much."

"Daisy, we appreciate everything you've done. Honestly, we wish it was more," Flo said. "Slim mentioned he hoped you'll consider taking a cordon bleu–level cooking course somewhere. Either this summer or after you finish college."

"The new chef at Wilder's said he was starting a cordon bleu class this summer," I told her. "Thank you so much." I wrapped my arms around her and gave her a big hug.

Flo squirmed away, but she had a big grin on her face. Her tattoos swirled and danced, like they were pulsating with happiness.

"Disgusting," I heard someone snort.

I'd heard that voice before, but I couldn't place it. I whipped my head around, but I couldn't tell who'd spoken.

There was one stranger in the restaurant though. She sat at the counter with an untouched cup of black coffee in front of her. She wore a wide scarf that covered her hair, enormous round sunglasses, and a white trench coat that covered most of her body. She looked like a celebrity who was trying to go in-cognito and failing. I was certain it was the same woman I'd seen with Sam's dad.

"We've had a lot of out-of-towners in the diner lately," I commented.

"It's been great for business," Flo said. "But there have been a few unusual customers."

It was like we'd been overrun by the CIA or something. Lots of women and men in dark suits and sunglasses, who sat in the corner and carried on low-voiced conversations, which they halted whenever someone approached them.

"Maybe they're paparazzi," I suggested. "After all, Circe is back in town."

She laughed. "Maybe."

I went back home to rearrange my cap and gown and to try on Grandma's graduation dress one more time.

Graduation day finally arrived.

The graduation ceremony was scheduled for indoors, in the gym at sundown, to allow the more nocturnal citizens to attend. We gathered in the drama room to don caps and gowns over our dressy attire. I wore Grandma's white dress with the daisies under my crimson robe but picked practical flats for my feet.

Despite the anticipation, our graduation went smoothly. I spotted Sam's father sitting a few rows ahead of my family. He was with the mystery woman I'd seen in the diner earlier.

As if she felt me staring at her, the woman turned around. I could sense her stare even through those dark sunglasses. Normally I didn't invade the thoughts of total strangers, but something about her bugged me, so I did a little fishing.

I'd just found her in the sea of thoughts when I very distinctly heard *Oh no you don't*, right before a blank wall slammed down and concealed her mind from mine. Startled, I turned my attention back to the ceremony. I'd been so busy trying to figure out who the woman was that I missed most of the valedictorian's speech. I was thrilled to see Lilah up there and tuned in just in time to hear her closing statement.

"To quote the great Dr. Seuss, 'The more that you read, the more things you will know. The more that you learn, the more places you'll go.'"

The audience laughed, and then when Lilah saw a few parents wiping away tears she said, "There's one more quote from the doctor that I'll leave you with. 'Don't cry because it's over. Smile because it happened.'"

Lilah received a standing ovation, and then it was finally time to get our diplomas. Mr. Amador called our names alphabetically, which meant Sam's name was called before mine. She received her diploma with her usual grace and gave the audience an impish smile as she turned her cap's tassel to the other side.

I, on the other hand, was my usual less-than-graceful self and nearly tripped going up on the stage.

I looked out into the audience and saw the faces of my family. Mom beamed proudly, and Dad made his best effort not to look sad and nearly blinded me with his hundred-watt smile. Nicholas and Rose clapped loudly, and I caught Poppy wiping away a tear when she didn't think anyone was looking. Grandma Giordano let out a piercing whistle as I shook hands with Principal Amador.

It was dark when the graduating class trooped outside for the traditional cap toss. I threw mine up in the air with a sense of accomplishment. I'd made it through high school. College would be a cinch after the things I'd been through. If I ever made it in, that is.

A bunch of people were invited back to our house for dinner. I'd invited Sean and Samantha, but her dad was taking Sean and his whole family to Chanticlair's, which was a very expensive restaurant in San Carlos.

Mom and Dad had made antipasto, cioppino, and fresh crusty bread.

"This looks delicious," Mr. Bone said.

Nicholas and Rose held hands under the table.

Liam and Poppy sat on opposite sides of the table, but he watched her with a goofy smile on his face

"Liam, how were finals?" I asked him.

He looked surprised that I had initiated a conversation with him, but answered politely. "Grueling," he said. "But Poppy made sure I put in enough study time."

I'd finally confessed to my parents about my lack of admittance, so it was a relief not to have to hide that I was pretty much a question mark until the UC Nightshade Admissions Office finally sent me a letter.

"I wonder how many other students are biting their nails?" Dad said as we sat around the table.

"Plenty," Chief Mendez said grimly. "There are at least a thousand students who haven't had their admittance to UC Nightshade finalized."

"Do they have any clues about who hacked the computer system?" Dad asked.

"They think it was someone who works there," Chief Mendez said.

"I have a mind to call and give someone a piece of my mind," Grandma said.

"It's okay," I said. "Something will work out. The new chef at Wilder's is starting up a cordon bleu program. Maybe I'll try that."

"I'll pay for new copper pots," Grandma said.

After we ate dinner, Dad said, "And now for the grand finale." He disappeared into the kitchen and came back wheeling a dessert cart with an enormous three-tiered cake. Frosting daisies cascaded down the sides, and CONGRATULATIONS, DAISY! was written in yellow on the top.

"That's why you guys shooed me out of the house," I said. "You two were baking my cake."

"It looks lovely, Mrs. Giordano," Liam said.

"Each layer is a different flavor," Mom said. "Let's cut into it."

Ryan and I took our cake and wandered out to the front porch. We sat in the swing and fed each other bites of cake. The perfect ending to a delicious dinner.

CHAPTER TWENTY-THREE

The next night was Grad Night, which was held at the Black Opal, an all-ages club in Santa Cruz. Half of Nightshade was going to be there. This year's event was supposed to be more spectacular than any in previous years.

We were lucky that the vampires and shifters had finally realized that neither side was responsible for the horrific death and attacks of the past few months. The arrest of the woman known as Trinity St. Claire did much to soothe the paranormal population.

Ryan picked me up early.

"Are you ready?" he asked.

"Yep," I said. "But I'm not sure if I can stay up all night."

He laughed. "We'll have to see about that."

"I hope they're serving coffee," I commented.

"They are," he said. "And beignets."

Grad Night had a New Orleans theme, and I was looking forward to some authentic Creole food. Slim was catering the event, and he'd been doing menu test runs at the café.

The other thing I liked is that I didn't have to dress up for the event. I was wearing my most comfortable pair of jeans, a cute top, and high-tops. At the last minute, I added the locket that Ryan had given me for my seventeenth birthday.

Ryan wore jeans, a dark green T-shirt, and sneakers.

"Are Sam and Sean riding with us?" he asked.

"They're meeting us there," I replied. "Sam had a last-minute wardrobe change to deal with."

The Black Opal had been transformed into New Orleans at Mardi Gras—that was clear from the full-size Mardi Gras float parked out front. I spotted my father's pink T-bird in the parking lot. It still made me cringe when I saw that car, but it made my father happy, so I couldn't bear to tell him its history.

My parents were at the front door with armloads of green, gold, and purple beads. My father draped a bunch of beads around my neck and then kissed my cheek. "Congratulations, graduate," he said. His voice wavered a little, but his smile was bright.

I gave him a hug. "I didn't know you were going to be here tonight."

He still didn't like to be in large crowds. Or around other people, except for immediate family, which was a result of his confinement at the hands of the Scourge.

"Are you kidding?" he said. "Nothing could keep me away."

"Thanks, Dad."

"We'll see you later," Mom said. "And have fun."

I grabbed Ryan's hand. "Can you believe this place?" I said.

"It's pretty cool," he admitted.

I spotted Samantha and Sean at a table with a bunch of the cheerleaders and their dates.

"Let's go talk to Sam," I said.

"You guys see each other all the time," Ryan protested, but with a smile. "When do I get a little alone time?"

"Later," I promised. I squeezed his hand. I'd find a way for a little alone time, even in a crowd this size. His stomach growled loudly. "We should feed you first," I said.

Rose and Nicholas were working the buffet. I spied Poppy and Liam and Grandma and the count, but I didn't see Ryan's dad anywhere.

"I thought your dad was going to be here."

He shrugged. "He said he had something to take care of. He'll be here."

"What do you want to try first?" I asked him.

"I've been thinking about those beignets all day," he said. "Let's eat dessert first."

"I could use a cup of coffee," I admitted.

We followed Ryan's nose toward the dessert bar, but before we could get there, Sam spotted us.

"Daisy!" Sam shrieked when she saw me. She ran over to us.

"Isn't it great?" she said, gesturing to the awesome spectacle of Grad Night. She wore a new pair of designer jeans and a purple top from the Tête de Mort boutique, along with about eight strings of beads around her neck.

At the dessert bar, I was shocked to see Circe Silvertongue frying up beignets. I knew she was up and around, but I had no idea she'd be at Grad Night.

"What is she doing here?" I hissed.

"I don't know," Ryan said. "Penance?"

When it was our turn in line, Circe handed me a beignet with a frosty smile. "Daisy."

"Circe," I said. "I'm not going to turn into a pig if I eat this, am I?"

"Only those who have truly hurt me become pigs," she said. "You, I would make an annoying little gadfly, which I would take great pleasure in squashing."

The little bit of pity I'd felt when she alluded to how much Balthazar had hurt her evaporated at her last comment.

"You have my pig," Circe said.

"He's *not* yours. Or a pig," I said. "At least, not for much longer."

Ryan took my hand. "Let's go before you say something you'll regret."

We sat around munching on delicious food, but dread gnawed at my brain. Something wasn't right. For one thing, I didn't recognize half of the Black Opal staff, and Ryan and I had been to the club many times to see Side Effects May Vary play.

"There's a mask-decorating station!" Ryan said. He dragged me over to the table and decorated a mask with huge bright green feathers, gold glitter, and fake pearls.

"Are you really going to wear that?" I laughed despite my worries.

"You bet," he said. He put it on and continued to wear it as we wove our way through the crowd.

Penny and Tyler were posing for photos underneath a giant purple and green balloon arch, so we went to have our photo taken too.

As we posed for the camera, Ryan put his hands on my shoulders and rubbed them. "Why so tense?" he said. "You've been edgy all night."

"I don't know," I said. "Sixth sense maybe?" I didn't want to ruin the evening by telling everyone that an inexplicable sense of dread had been building since I walked into the Black Opal.

Sam overheard us. "Should we add premonition to your powers, Daisy?"

I forced a laugh. "Of course not," I said. "I'm just being foolish. I'm so used to things going wrong that I don't know how to cope when they don't."

A four-piece jazz band started playing on the main stage,

and we drifted over to watch them. There was so much to do and see and eat that I didn't think I'd have much trouble staying awake after all.

A bunch of little kids were there, volunteering with their parents. Sean's sisters and his parents were all working the ring-the-bell strong-man game, and we went over to say hi.

"Show me how strong you are," I teased Ryan.

He picked up one of the mallets and struck a pose, flexing his considerable muscle.

All of Sean's little sisters giggled at his antics, even Jessica.

I'd finally shaken my bad mood, shedding it like a second skin, and I was able to enjoy our graduation party. Even overhearing Penny Edwards's mom bragging about Penny's admittance to Arizona State didn't pop my happy bubble.

"What do you want to do now?" I asked Ryan.

My boyfriend whisked me into a dark corner. "This," he said. He gave me a sweet kiss and then another. We passed a very enjoyable half hour before I put a hand to his chest. "We should get back to the party," I said. "Mom and Dad are chaperoning, and they'll freak out if they notice I'm gone."

He sighed. "I guess you're right. I just got back into your dad's good graces."

We rejoined the party and hit the candy buffet, which was exactly what it sounded like. Every sweet imaginable in the Mardi Gras colors of green, purple, and gold.

We each took a cupful of candy and sat down at a table with Penny, Tyler, Sean, and Samantha. The feeling I'd been trying to ignore for weeks was back again, building inside me, no matter how hard I tried to shove it away and just be happy.

"I'm going outside for a breath of fresh air," I told Ryan quietly.

"I'll go with you," he replied.

"No, it's okay," I said. "I just need a second or two of quiet. The noise in here is getting to be too much for me." I slipped outside.

I saw Spenser Devereaux move stealthily in the parking lot. He was acting weird, like he didn't want anyone to notice what he was doing. I looked around, but nobody else seemed to think it was odd. On impulse, I followed him.

He made his way to his car, a newer-model BMW, which was parked near my father's pink pride and joy. He glanced around, and I ducked into the shadows, feeling slightly foolish. He was probably just getting something out of his car.

I started to turn away, but then curiosity got the better of me. What was he getting? A graduation present for Sam?

It was hard to see in the dark, but I heard him chuckling to himself as he popped the trunk. Then he walked to my dad's car and fumbled with a key ring before inserting a key into the trunk of the T-bird. After he popped the trunk, Mr. Devereaux went back to his BMW, picked up something heavy wrapped in what looked like trash bags, and dumped it into my dad's car. He had to shove the package down before the trunk lid would close.

Then he rubbed his hands together and chuckled diabolically. He scanned the parking lot, and I stood as still as I could, hoping that my cover held and he wouldn't spot me. Seemingly satisfied that he hadn't been observed, he stripped off the gloves he'd been wearing and threw them into the Dumpster. He chuckled again, and the sound sent chills down my spine. He didn't sound like the man I'd known my whole life.

What was going on? Was this some weird prank or something more sinister?

I waited a long time after he left before I finally released the breath I didn't even know I'd been holding. I returned to the club, slipping in the back, through the kitchen entrance.

Natalie gave me a distracted wave, but Rose sent a message my way. *Are you okay?*

I shook my head. *I just saw something weird. Mr. Devereaux—*

The thought was cut off when Ryan came striding toward me. "I've been looking for you everywhere," he said. "I should have known to look in the kitchen."

"Sorry," I said. "Hey, is your dad here yet?" The chief would know what to do. I was already questioning whether or not I'd seen what I thought I'd seen. Mr. Devereaux was Sam's dad and my father's friend. But he'd seemed like a completely different person out there.

Ryan frowned and looked at his watch. "No," he said. "And he's been gone for hours and hasn't checked in with me. That's not like him."

A thought occurred to me. I had seen Officer Denton with his fiancée at the buffet line about an hour ago. Maybe he could help. "I'll be right back," I told Ryan.

On the way, I spotted my mom conversing with one of her friends from work.

"Mom, I need to talk to you about something," I said. I had to raise my voice in order to be heard over their conversation. I noticed the frown on her face and added, "I'm sorry to interrupt, but it's important."

"Please excuse me for a moment, Joyce," Mom said. We went into the hallway by the bathrooms, where it was a little less noisy.

I explained to her what I'd seen. "Mom, it was just so weird," I said. "And it looked like a body he was stuffing in there." I shivered at the thought.

"Did you tell Chief Mendez?" she asked.

"I want to," I said. "But he's not here yet."

"What?" she said. "He left the station hours ago."

I had a very bad feeling in my stomach. I realized then what it was I'd actually witnessed.

"Mom, Dad needs us," I said.

I ran outside without waiting to see if she followed. Officer Denton and my father were looking at something in the open trunk of my father's pink convertible. They both had horrified expressions. Mr. Devereaux stood off to one side, but I thought I detected a smirk on his face. I nearly threw up when I saw a leg dangling from the trunk. Somehow I knew the person that leg belonged to was dead. I took in the scene, and in an instant I knew what had happened. Spenser Devereaux was framing my father for murder, and Officer Denton was buying it. He said something, and my father put his hands behind his back so the officer could cuff him. Panic set in as I streaked toward them.

"Rafe Giordano, you are under arrest for the murder of Chief Mendez. You have the right to remain silent. Anything you say—"

"No!" I said. The force of my protest sent Officer Denton flying against the car.

"Daisy, it's okay," my dad said. "Calm down."

I inhaled and then exhaled several times, trying to do as he asked.

"It's not okay," I replied. "The reality of what Officer Denton had said sunk in, and my stomach gave an awful heave. "No," I said again. No, it couldn't be. Not the chief. Not . . . Ryan's dad.

"My father didn't do it, and I can prove it," I said. I relayed what I'd seen Sam's dad do.

Mr. Devereaux looked at his watch. "I'm afraid I don't have time for this," he said.

I added, "He threw his gloves in the Dumpster over there." That wiped the smirk from the professor's face.

CHAPTER TWENTY-FOUR

Sam chose the worst possible moment to come outside.

"What's going on?" she asked, looking from one of us to the next in puzzlement.

"It's nothing, Samantha," the professor said. "Go back inside."

"It's not nothing," I said hotly. "Chief Mendez is dead."

"I don't understand," she said. "What's happening? Why is your father in handcuffs?"

"Sam," I said. "Your dad . . ." There wasn't an easy way to say it. "He killed Chief Mendez and tried to frame my father."

Officer Denton came back with a pair of gloves in an evidence bag.

"No!" Sam screamed. "No! Daddy, tell them it's not true." The look on Samantha's face confirmed that she had been as oblivious as I was. It was worse than I had ever imagined.

To my relief, Officer Denton took the cuffs off my father's wrists. "Think about it, Samantha," I said. "His weird disappearances? The woman with the birthmark? We both saw her that night, and then she was caught trying to poison everyone at Slim's."

I saw the exact second when realization dawned in her face.

"These people are my friends, Dad," Samantha said. "I can't believe you've been plotting to hurt them for all these years."

"Ridding the world of vermin is expensive, but it's worth every penny," he said. "And I eventually found a way to recoup some of my losses." He grinned evilly.

"You mean, illegally?" she asked.

"I did it for you, Samantha," he said. "To make the world safe for you to live in."

"What about Chief Mendez?" she said.

"It was necessary," he said.

"Necessary?" she screamed at him. "Necessary? He was Ryan's father. You killed Sean's best friend's dad. He was a good person."

"He was a Were. Vermin." The disgust in her father's voice made Sam start to cry.

Mr. Devereaux was telling us an awful lot for a criminal. It was almost like he didn't think it would matter.

Mr. Bone stepped out of the shadows. His normally smiling face looked grim as he grabbed Mr. Devereaux by the arm. "Come with me, Devereaux."

"What is this? A citizen's arrest?" Mr. Devereaux scoffed.

"Not exactly," Mr. Bone said. The look in his eyes made Mr. Devereaux cringe. "Officer Denton," Mr. Bone continued, "please arrest this man." Mr. Devereaux was lucky that Mr. Bone was a law-abiding citizen.

Sam collapsed into my arms as her father was cuffed by Officer Denton. Tightly.

Strangely, there was a smirk on Mr. Devereaux's face. "I'm sure your graduation party will be a major blowout," he called out as the officer led him away.

What did he mean by that?

Mr. Bone and my parents followed them, and then it was silent, except for the sound of my best friend's pain.

"Shhh," I said. "It'll be okay. It'll be okay." I was trying to convince myself as much as Sam. How could it be okay? Ryan's dad had been murdered. It couldn't get worse than that, could it?

Then a terrified scream echoed in my mind. I looked around to make sure I hadn't heard it, and there was silence, except for the sound of Sam's sobs. I glanced over at the Black Opal. It was completely dark. Something was wrong. The power had been cut.

"Sam," I said. "I need you to be strong now."

She sniffed. "But my father . . ."

"Something's wrong," I said. "Something is terribly wrong. I heard a scream."

My words drew her out of her own misery for a moment. "I didn't hear anything."

"I know," I replied. Sometimes I forgot that not everyone had powers like mine.

I sent a message to my sister. *Rose, is everything all right inside?*

Inside? Where are you?

Never mind that. Are you okay?

The power just went off.

Something Mr. Devereaux had said finally sank in. The graduation party would be a blowout. Would he actually be crazy enough to endanger his own daughter? I started to shake when I realized the answer.

You need to get everyone out of there now.

WHAT? WHY?

Please, Rose, just do it. I think the Scourge plans an explosion. Get everyone out of there! We'll be there to help in a minute.

No, stay there.

There was no way I was going to follow her advice.

"Sam, I have to go inside for a minute," I said. "But no matter what, don't come in after me, do you hear me?"

"Daisy, what's going on?"

The dread on my face answered her question.

"Something bad," she said with certainty. "And my dad's responsible. I'm going with you."

"Sam," I protested.

"Sean's in there," she said, her voice trembling. "And the rest of his family, including Katie. How could he do that?"

I couldn't say no. "Let's go," I said. "But stay close to me no matter what. And keep a lookout for the members of the Scourge."

"What do they look like?" Sam asked.

"You'll know 'em when you see 'em," I said. "They'll be the ones trying to kill us."

We approached the front door, which was blocked. A huge silver bar was wedged through the door handles, preventing anyone from escaping.

A pudgy middle-aged man was guarding the entrance.

He didn't seem to notice me at all, as his entire attention was focused on Samantha. He grinned evilly and stepped into Sam's personal space.

"Late to the party are you, princess?" He was busy with Samantha, which meant I could use my powers of telekinesis to unlock the door. It was tougher than I thought, but I tried to remember Poppy's coaching and finally managed to get one end of the bar to wiggle a little.

"Hands off, you moron," Sam said.

I whipped my head around and saw that the creep had his hands all over Samantha.

"What do you think you're doing?" I said.

"He obviously doesn't know who my dad is," Sam said. She gave him a shove, and he released her.

"Who's your daddy?" the man leered, but he sounded worried. Good.

"Spenser Devereaux," she said. "The leader of the Scourge."

"What?" the man said. He sounded caught off-guard, maybe even a little scared. "The boss didn't say anything about his daughter being here."

It looked like he was buying Sam's story, so I returned my attention back to the bars.

"He must have forgotten," she lied convincingly.

I finally managed to free the bar. It hovered in the air, but I couldn't get it to move.

"Let me call it in," the man said. He reached for his phone. That's when the bar flew through the air and smacked him across the face. He fell to the ground.

"It took you long enough," Sam said. "That guy had breath as bad as a zombie's."

"Is he breathing?"

She stepped over him. "Would it be so bad if he wasn't? Let's go rescue our friends."

Inside, it was chaos. Members of the Scourge were locked in combat with the citizens of Nightshade, paranormal and normal alike.

Sam disappeared for a minute and I panicked, wondering if she'd already been snatched by one of the Scourge.

They weren't really trying to do much damage, I noticed. There were no guns or serious weapons. They were just trying to keep everyone inside, until the explosion.

Bane carried a bleeding Mrs. Wilder as Elise and Wolfgang forged a trail by knocking down anyone who got in their way.

Sam reappeared at my side. "There's Katie!" she said.

Jessica carried Katie as the rest of the Walsh sisters trailed behind. I flinched when I saw a short red-haired man move toward them. Jessica put Katie down behind her and then grabbed a nearby folding chair. She brought it down on his head, and the man crumpled to the ground. A tattoo stood out in stark relief on her arm and then faded away.

As they moved toward the exit, a large blond woman stepped into their path and raised her fists. Before she could strike, Samantha launched herself at the woman and tackled her to the floor.

"Come with me," I said to the girls.

Sam was still smacking the woman with her purse. "Sam, let's go. We need to get the girls out of here and then find Sean and Ryan."

With one last thump from Sam, the woman passed out.

Sam smiled in satisfaction and then shouldered her purse again.

"What do you have in there, rocks?" I asked her as we moved through the crowd. Jessica had picked Katie back up and the rest of Sean's sisters followed.

"Even better," she said. "I loaded it up with rolls of quarters from the ring-toss booth."

All around us, Nightshade citizens were doing battle with the Scourge.

Flo was a whirring, kicking blur. She seemed to be everywhere at once.

"I didn't know she could fight like that," I said. A voice at my ear said, "She's a virago, Daisy. A woman warrior whose powers are only activated when the city is in peril."

"Slim! You're okay," I said, relieved. "A virago, huh?"

I filed the information away for later. I was fairly certain there was a virago in Sean's family, one who would be starting high school in the fall.

Natalie was on his other side, but she didn't speak to me. She was reciting a chant, and I was relieved when I realized it was a protective spell for the little kids.

The few times she got close enough, I saw that Flo's tattoos were swirling as she moved.

"Can you take the girls and get them out of here? As far from the club as you can go?" I asked Slim. "Sam, you go with them."

"Absolutely," he said. "I'll take them to the restaurant. I have my catering van. They should be safe there. Please watch out for my sister."

"I'll do my best," I said. But he and the girls were already gone.

CHAPTER TWENTY-FIVE

When I turned around, Dr. Franken was right in front of me. She was the professor who had created and set loose doppelgangers of Nightshade residents.

Her snowy white hair had been dyed sunflower yellow, and I finally realized who the woman in the white trench coat, scarf, and sunglasses had been. She'd probably been just waiting for a chance to take a swing at me. Her next words confirmed my suspicion.

"You don't know how long I've been waiting to do this," she said.

She came at me with one of the strong-man mallets. Instinctively, I put up a hand to shield my face—I didn't think to try using my powers.

There was a cold blast of air from somewhere behind me. It passed by me and hit Dr. Franken with an icy accuracy. She stood rooted to the spot, frozen. I turned around.

Circe stood there, eyes still shooting green sparks.

"Thank you," I said as she walked over to me.

"I would not allow one of the Scourge scum to kill you," she said. "That pleasure I reserve for myself one day, if I so choose." She put out one elegant long finger and pushed over the ice sculpture that used to be Dr. Franken. The statue hit the floor with a thump and shattered into a billion little pieces.

I spotted Rose and Nicholas at the other end of the room. They were herding a group of the younger kids. I assumed they were heading for the emergency exit near the bathrooms.

I sent a message. *Slim and Sam are taking the kids to his restaurant. They should be safe there. Where's Poppy?*

She's with Liam. Fighting.

Not much time, I warned her. I was sure that whatever was going to happen was going to happen at midnight. The witching hour. I saw her nod, then she said something to Nicholas and they disappeared from my line of sight.

The Scourge had figured out that the front exit was no longer barred. A dozen or so people formed a human chain in front of the door.

Liam and his grandfather approached them with lightning-quick speed but were repelled when the group held out large crosses.

I concentrated as hard as I could, and the crosses flew out of their hands and over the heads of the vampires, finally landing in a corner. I hoped they'd stay there.

"Get the psychic," one of them shouted.

Penny Edwards came through the crowd with a bunch of the cheerleaders. Jordan jumped on the back of a woman who was carrying a flamethrower. Penny threw a handful of beads at one of the Scourge, and they turned into hissing snakes. He recoiled in terror and ran from the room.

Liam had been wounded. I could see cross-shaped boils rising on his face, but he continued to fight.

Lilah Porter dove into the dunk tank. A second later, she flipped her tail, opened her mouth, and started to sing.

Rose, tell Nicholas to cover his ears. Liam too.

What?

Lilah's singing.

A haunting melody filled the room, and soon the males, Scourge and paranormal alike, were mesmerized by the sound and threw down their weapons. Lilah Porter's song of enchantment was working. One of the members of the Scourge caught on after he saw Nicholas covering his ears. The Scourge agent, an overweight man with a WHAT WOULD DEVEREAUX DO T-shirt on, put his hands over his ears and then motioned to the others to do the same. Then they all ran. The club was nearly empty, but there was still no sign of Ryan. I couldn't be sure, but I thought that everyone had gotten out in time. I wasn't leaving without him, no matter what.

I looked at the clock. Its hands were pointed perilously close to twelve. I knew it would suit Mr. Devereaux's twisted psyche to have the explosion go off promptly at midnight.

"Ryan," I said, scanning the room. "Where's Ryan?"

I saw a flash of green feathers. Ryan's mask. He had fallen to the floor. He was almost obscured by the wreckage from the battle. He was slumped over, leaning with his back against the bar. He was also bleeding profusely from his arm.

"Silver bullet," he said. "It's lucky he missed my heart."

Gun? I hadn't seen any guns.

"Can you believe it?" Ryan said. "Wait until my dad finds out."

His words gave me a terrible pang. He didn't know. So much had happened in the last hour, but there was no time to tell him of his father's death. At least, not until we were safely out of the Black Opal and far away.

"We need to get you out of here and to a hospital." He'd lost a lot of blood, and besides, unless I'd guessed wrong, things were about to get even uglier.

I bent down and put his good arm around my neck. "We have to move you. I'm pretty sure there's going to be an explosion. This is going to hurt."

I tried moving Ryan magically, but my powers decided at the worst possible moment not to cooperate. It was going to be good old-fashioned muscle or nothing. I gave a desperate heave and with Ryan's help managed to get him on his feet.

We were the only two people left in the building. We

headed for the door, but as we reached it, there was a deafening roar. A voice in my head screamed. Then I realized the voice I heard was my own. There was a sharp pain to my head, and everything went black.

CHAPTER TWENTY-SIX

When I woke up, the first thing I saw was ugly wallpaper in an unfamiliar room. Then the worried faces of my parents swam into focus.

"Where am I?" I tried to sit up, but the pain in my head wouldn't let me. "What happened?"

Although my eyesight was a little blurry, I didn't miss the look they exchanged. "What do you remember?"

"Grad Night, the Scourge, Ryan getting shot," I said. "Ryan! Where is he?"

"I'm right here," he said soothingly. I tried to swivel my head around, but the pain started again. "Don't move," he said as he appeared in my line of sight. I didn't see any signs of major injury other than a cut on his face that was already healing and a sling on his arm.

"Were blood speeds healing," he said.

I was grateful for his physical recuperation, but he looked worn, like a light had gone out somewhere in his soul.

Then it all came rushing back to me. Chief Mendez was

dead. No wonder Ryan looked so sad. I reached over and squeezed his hand. "I'm so sorry," I said.

He squeezed my hand back but wouldn't look me in the eyes. "Dad found out that Trinity wasn't the leader of the Scourge," he said, "but he had never expected it to be Mr. Devereaux."

Dad grimaced. "I wish I had remembered sooner," he said. "I told the chief that I remembered Trinity and that she had been with someone I knew. We were at the university. It was late. Someone offered me a cup of coffee. It must have been drugged. I had no idea it was Spenser. I thought he was my friend."

"No one knew," I said. *Except Lily.* Why hadn't I told anyone about Lil's musical clue?

"My dad figured it out," Ryan said, "when I told him about the jukebox songs."

"Sam's dad had been spending a lot of money," I said.

Dad nodded. "That was a tipoff too. Spenser told everyone that he was rich again because of his book. But it was really the Scourge's criminal activities that made him wealthy. What finally gave Spenser away was that he got too greedy and hacked the college computers. They were able to determine that the criminal had done it using a faculty password. And it was fairly easy to monitor his bank accounts. He had way too much money for a college professor, even one with a book deal."

"How did he get all that money?" I wondered.

Dad shrugged. "Identity theft. Fraud. Plain old theft. And donations from wealthy, like-minded individuals."

I shuddered. "I can't believe it was Mr. Devereaux the whole time. What if there's someone else who will just step into his shoes and start running the Scourge?"

"If it's any comfort, Mr. Bone believes that most of the top leaders have been arrested."

"Poor Samantha. How is she taking it?"

"Badly," Mom said.

Part of me felt like we were playing Twenty Questions, but I just couldn't stop. I had to know everything that had happened.

I put a hand to my head and felt a thick bandage. "What's wrong with me?"

Dad cleared his throat and tried to sound cheerful. "You're fine," he said. "You had to have a few stitches though. And you'll have a sore head for a day or two."

"Did everyone make it out of the Black Opal before the explosion?" I asked. "It was an explosion, right?"

"We'll talk about that later," Mom said. "Samantha and your sisters want to see you for a few minutes, and then you need to take a nap."

I was stiff and sore. "I feel like I've been sleeping for days," I said.

There was that look again.

Ryan gave me a goodbye kiss and they all left, and a few minutes later my two sisters took their places by my hospital bed.

"There's a huge crowd outside," Rose said. "Everyone is waiting to see you, but we wanted to talk to you alone."

"Are you going to tell me what's really going on?" I asked.

"They're worried you lost your psychic skills after all," Poppy said, then clapped her hand over her mouth. Leave it to Poppy to spill the beans.

"That's what has Mom and Dad all freaked out?"

"That and the fact that you were still in the building when the whole thing went up in a ball of flames," Poppy said.

"How did we get out?" I asked. "The last thing I remember is that Ryan had been shot and we were trying to escape."

"Ryan," Rose said succinctly, "carried you out."

"But he could barely stand when I found him," I replied. Parts of the night were coming back to me.

"Inhuman werewolf strength," Poppy said.

"How about Nicholas?" I asked Rose. "And Liam?"

"They're both fine," she replied. "Liam has a burn from where a cross touched him, but he's okay."

"The chief," I said. "Is he really dead? It wasn't just some scheme to catch the real head of the Scourge?"

"He's really gone," Rose said. "I'm so sorry, Daisy."

"When's the . . . the funeral?"

"You were unconscious a long time," Poppy said carefully.

I stared at her. "How long?"

"Three days," Rose said.

"I've been out for *three days?*" That explained the weird looks.

"They already had the funeral. Everyone from Nightshade came."

"Poor Ryan," I said.

"His grandmother came from Orange County," Poppy said. "She's staying at the house with him for now."

"What's he going to do?" I said. Ryan and his dad had been super close. I could only imagine what he was feeling right now.

I kicked the covers off and swung my feet out of bed.

"Oh no you don't," Rose said. "Mom would kill us."

"I can't stay in bed for one second longer," I replied.

"You're going to stay in there for as long as the doctors tell you to," Poppy said sternly.

I made a face at her.

"Mom and Dad were really worried," Rose said. "Ryan was beside himself. We're just lucky it wasn't a full moon. I swear he would have taken this place apart."

"I'll stay put," I said. "For now."

"How is Sam?" I asked.

"She's in the hallway, waiting to see you," Poppy said. "In fact, we should get out of here so she can come in."

My sisters left, and then Sam, Jordan, and Sean came

in. Sam's eyes were red-rimmed, but her smile was as bright as ever.

"I'm sorry," she said. "I know you probably don't want to be my friend anymore, not after what my dad did, but I'm sorry."

"It's not your fault," I said. "I would never think it was your fault."

"I wasn't paying attention," she said tearfully. "All those clues that there was something strange going on with my own father, and I didn't even care."

"Samantha, nobody blames you," Jordan said.

She ignored Jordan like she hadn't even spoken. "You know the worst part?" Sam continued. "I still love him, even though I know all the horrible things he did. Kidnapping your father, k-k-killing Ryan's dad." She burst into sobs, and Jordan wrapped her arms around her.

"Samantha Devereaux, you listen to me," I said sternly. "Of course you love him. He's your father. That doesn't mean you agree with what he did."

She threw herself into my arms. I winced, but ignored the pain and patted her back consolingly.

Sam pulled herself together. "Thanks, Daisy," she said.

After they left, there was a steady stream of visitors to my room until finally a nurse ushered everyone out of the room and I fell into a deep sleep.

CHAPTER TWENTY-SEVEN

A few weeks after the Grad Night disaster, things were slowly returning to normal. I was working a shift at Slim's, and Ryan sat at the counter, keeping me company.

Rose and Nicholas were hanging out with Liam and Poppy. From the sound of their laughter, the four of them were getting along great.

Lil, however, was sulking. She played "Broken Promises" by Survivor and "You Let Me Down" by Billie Holiday over and over again. Natalie had tried again to reverse the spell, but it hadn't worked. She wasn't giving up, but it looked like her magic just wasn't strong enough to free Balthazar and Lily.

Mr. Bone rushed into the diner. "I have the most wonderful news," he said.

For a second, I thought he was going to tell me that they had made a horrible mistake and Ryan's dad wasn't really dead, but that didn't happen.

"Circe Silvertongue has agreed to reverse the spell," he declared.

"Circe has reformed?" I asked.

"Not exactly," Mr Bone replied. "But she's finally ready to undo her wickedness."

"What changed her mind? Guilt? Pity?" I guessed.

He cleared his throat. "She was persuaded to revisit this issue by her new husband."

"Husband? You mean, Circe got married? Who?" Who would be brave or foolhardy enough to take on Circe Silver-tongue voluntarily?

I answered my own question, suddenly realizing who her new husband was. "Count Dracul." Liam's grandfather was married to the meanest woman I'd ever met—and I'd met quite a few of them in the course of my investigations.

"After she reverses the spell, the count is taking her on a trip to Europe for their honeymoon," Mr. Bone said.

I couldn't say I would miss her. "When?" I asked. Lily and Balthazar would finally be free.

"They will be here shortly," he said.

"Where's Balthazar?" I said.

"Balthazar's in the back with Natalie," Flo said. "I'm going to put the Closed sign up before any customers show up."

I shredded a paper napkin into tiny pieces. Ryan reached out and took my hand.

"Don't worry, Daisy," he said. "She'll keep her promise."

"She'd better," I muttered. After such a horrible gradua-tion day, I wanted this to work, now more than ever. I didn't think I could bear it if anything went wrong.

Circe swept into the restaurant, followed by Count Dracul. Natalie and Balthazar emerged from the back, curious.

"Let's get this over with," Circe said. "Darling, place the pig next to the jukebox."

The sight of the normally fastidious count carrying a pet pig was so incongruous that it almost made me laugh.

The count put Balthazar down gently, and the pig trotted over to the jukebox and nuzzled the cold surface with his snout.

Lil started to play "Crying" by Roy Orbison, and then the song began to skip. It sounded almost like Lil was the one doing the crying.

Circe ignored the distraction. "You have the objects?" she asked me.

I nodded. "I'll be right back," I said.

Slim had been keeping the ring and the pen in the restaurant safe. He carefully unlocked the safe and said the magic word that Natalie had given us. In true lovebird fashion, the magic word was *wedding*, which I thought was terribly cute.

I came back with the items, and Circe held out her hand imperiously. I gave her Balthazar's pen and Lily's engagement ring, even though part of me still didn't trust her.

She seemed to forget all about everyone around her. She sank to her knees and went into a deep trance. Unlike Natalie,

Circe spoke no words aloud, but I could see her lips moving. After several minutes, her eyes regained their focus.

Count Dracul helped her up. She steadied herself and then dusted off her hands. "It is done," she said.

She turned her brilliant green eyes on me. "Someone," she emphasized, "has been interfering with my magic."

"We were just trying to break the spell," I said. I didn't mention that Natalie had added a little spell of her own.

There was silence in the diner while we waited for something, anything, to happen. But nothing did.

And then the jukebox kicked in with a song.

"It didn't work," I said. I was so disappointed that I wanted to cry.

"Of course it worked," Circe said haughtily. "It isn't like fast food, you imbecile."

I opened my mouth to say something to her, but the count took her by the hand and led her away for a moment. He said something to her so softly that I couldn't hear. But whatever he said worked, because Circe came back to me. "My apologies," she said stiffly. "It has been pointed out to me that not everyone knows how such advanced magic works."

"Listen to the song," Ryan said softly.

"Never Forget You" by the Noisettes came on. My attention had been on the jukebox, but Balthazar squealed and I whipped my head around to stare at him.

231

The pig's body shook, and suddenly Balthazar the pig was gone and in his place was a young man. He had curly black hair and a moustache and, I was happy to see, was fully dressed in a black tuxedo. I assumed that was what he'd been wearing when his enchantment began.

I could tell Circe was surprised to see the man she used to love looking so young and handsome.

"Bam, is it really you?" she said. "You look like you haven't aged a bit." She didn't sound particularly happy about the last part.

He opened his mouth, but nothing came out except a tiny squeal. "Where am I?" he finally said. His voice sounded rusty from disuse.

"You're in Nightshade," she said. "You've been gone a long time."

He gave her a cold look. "I remember being a pig. Where is my fiancée? Where is Lily?"

But there was still no sign of Lily Varcol.

"I have done what I agreed to do," Circe said. She looked at the count when she said it.

"Yes, my dear, you have," Count Dracul said. "And now I will keep my promise to you and show you the wonders of Paris."

He gave Poppy a low bow and kissed her hand. "Take good care of my grandson," he said.

"I will," she said.

Then Circe swept from the room in the same haughty way she had entered. The count came up to me. "Daisy Giordano, it has been a pleasure to meet you," he said. "I expect great things from you. You have the heart of a lion."

"Th-thank you," I said.

After another low bow, he departed without a backward glance.

Ryan and I exchanged a look. "Was that a compliment?" I asked.

"Yes, I believe it was," he replied.

The jukebox had gone silent but suddenly kicked in again. Lil played "I'll be There" by the Jackson Five.

"What a great song," I said. "But I really hoped that the spell would work for both of them." I glanced over at Bam, who looked forlorn in his tuxedo. All dressed up and no one to dance with.

Then a silver shimmer appeared, hovering above the jukebox. It hung suspended in the air and slowly floated to the ground. As it did, the shimmering shape materialized into a solid form. A young woman in a long white gown was standing in Slim's Diner. She looked bewildered, but I recognized her from the painting I'd seen at the Wilder estate when I first discovered that Lily Varcol had disappeared.

She ignored everyone else in the room to focus on her fiancé. "Bam, is that really you?"

233

He swept her into his arms and kissed her so long that I had to turn away from all the raw emotion I sensed in their embrace.

I sighed. Lily Varcol was finally reunited with her one true love.

Ryan grabbed my hand and gave it a squeeze. "You did a good thing," he said.

"Mrs. Wilder!" I said. "We need to call her and get her down here."

"Go gently," Flo advised. "She's had a rough time lately."

"I'll call Bane," Ryan said. "And he and Elise can ease Mrs. Wilder into it."

"Good idea," I said.

We drifted over to a booth to allow Lily and Bam a little privacy.

"Anyone hungry?" Slim asked.

Natalie said, "I'm starving."

"I could eat," Ryan said.

He was a werewolf. He could always eat.

A little while later, Bane, Elise, and Mrs. Wilder came into the restaurant. Mrs. Wilder was white with excitement and shock.

"Is she okay?" I asked Elise. She nodded. Elise could speak now, but it was difficult for her, and her voice had been changed forever by the attack.

Mrs. Wilder approached her sister slowly and leaned on her cane.

Lily realized that someone was staring at her and broke free of Bam's embrace. She looked Mrs. Wilder up and down for a long moment and then broke into noisy sobs. "Hilda, is that really you?" she said, once she regained her composure. "You're so . . . old."

Mrs. Wilder put out a trembling hand and touched her sister's face. "I am," she said. "But by some miracle, you are just the same as you were when you left."

Lily put a hand to her own face and felt the smoothness of her cheek. "How is that possible?"

Bam took her hand. "Fortune was kind, my love. We have the rest of our lives to spend together."

"Your house," Mrs. Wilder said, then cleared her throat. "Merriweather House is just as you left it," she told Bam.

"We can have the wedding there," he said to Lily. "If you'll still have me."

"Try to stop me," she replied.

Mrs. Wilder drew Elise forward. "This is my granddaughter, Elise." If Elise thought it was weird that her great-aunt looked almost as young as she was, she didn't act it.

Lily held out her hand to shake Elise's.

"Pleased to meet you," she said.

"Your ring," Bam said. "Where is your ring?"

"Circe used it to work the enchantment," I explained. I handed it to Bam, who immediately slipped it on his fiancée's finger.

She admired it for a long moment, a happy smile on her lips.

"I've been in a dream for so long," Lily said. "I played music, but no one heard me. But then there was a girl who finally listened."

"Daisy," Natalie said. "You mean Daisy."

I clung to Ryan's hand and tried not to cry. I couldn't believe that it was finally happening, that my friend Lil was finally free.

"Yes, Daisy," Lily said. "Where is she?"

"I'm here," I said in a small voice.

Lily rushed to me and gave me a long hug. I could smell her perfume. "I owe you so much," she said.

"I owe you," I said. "All those cases you helped me with. All those mysteries we solved together."

Part of me was sad that I didn't have my prophetic jukebox to turn to in times of crisis. Nightshade had changed irrevocably in the last few weeks.

"I'll still be there for you," she said softly. "Anytime you need anything, you can stop by Merriweather House and talk to me."

"I will," I said.

"And you're all invited to the wedding," Bam said. He gave Lily a fond smile. "I'm not willing to wait much longer, darling."

She nodded. "Let's get married as soon as possible. I think we have set the record for the world's longest engagement."

Everyone laughed at that, even Mrs. Wilder, who still seemed slightly dazed by the recent turn of events.

"This calls for a celebration," Slim said. He came out carrying a tray full of drinks. Lily and Bam didn't even bat an eye at his appearance, or lack thereof. I guess it was to be expected, since they'd spent years as a jukebox and a pig, respectively.

We toasted to Balthazar and Lily, to Natalie and Slim, and, finally, to true love.

"We have so much to do," Mrs. Wilder said. "A wedding to plan."

Samantha and Sean came in the door of the diner a few minutes later. She had a stack of papers clutched in her hand.

"You're not going to believe this," she said. She gulped. "We were going through my dad's things in his office. Look what I found!" She waved a stack of envelopes frantically in my face.

I tried to read the lettering on the envelopes, but she was still waving them. "Sam, what are they?"

"Acceptance letters," she said. "*Your* acceptance letters."

"Why would your dad have my mail?" I said. Then I recalled Trinity masquerading as my mail carrier.

She hesitated. "I know he was trying to stop your dad from publishing his book," she said.

"Yes, we figured that after—"

"After his arrest." She met my eyes. "It's okay, Daisy. You can say it."

"But what does that have to do with our mail?"

"A lot," Rose said. "Dad sent his manuscript out via the post office. So Mr. Devereaux probably hoped to intercept his correspondence or his manuscript and see exactly what Dad remembered about his abduction."

"This one is from UC Nightshade," Sam said.

"Open it!" Poppy said.

I took a deep breath and ran my finger along the edge. "Wish me luck," I said to the waiting crowd of friends and family.

I opened the crisp stationery and read, "We are pleased to inform you . . ."

Poppy's screeching drowned out the rest of my words, but everyone got the general idea.

"I've been accepted," I said. "But this letter is over two months old. What if they didn't hold a place for me?"

"I'm sure they did," Rose said reassuringly. "If not, maybe you can attend part-time this fall."

I tried to swallow my worry. I smiled at Slim and Flo. "A certain boss of mine did give me a wonderful opportunity to take more cooking lessons."

"It'll work out," Poppy said.

College was no longer my big looming fear, nor was being apart from Ryan. We were all lucky to be alive, even though Ryan's father hadn't been so lucky.

I looked over at the jukebox and decided to put in a few quarters for old times' sake. I held my breath when I punched in the numbers, but my selections came on. No random song choices, no hidden messages, no Lil.

"It's just a jukebox now," I told Ryan.

After closing, everyone eventually drifted off, but Ryan and I stayed at Slim's, not talking.

Finally, he stirred. "Want to go for a drive?"

I wondered if this was when he was going to tell me goodbye. Nightshade would hold only painful memories for him now.

"Won't your grandma worry?" I asked.

"She went home yesterday," Ryan said. "I'll see her soon though."

I was convinced that he was going to leave Nightshade and live with his grandma until college started in the fall.

He parked his car near the highest point in Nightshade, and we walked hand in hand to the top of the outlook. There was a sliver of a moon in the sky. I looked down on the town.

"I wanted to tell you first," he said.

My heart ended up somewhere on the ground at his words.

"Tell me what?"

"I'm not going to go to school in Orange County," he said. "I'm staying right here in Nightshade. I know what I want to do now. I want to be a police officer. Like my dad."

"Are you sure?" I said.

He nodded and gulped back tears.

"Your dad would have been so proud of you," I said. I brushed a tear of my own away.

Ryan put his arm around me. "We'll be all right," he said. "No matter what."

Our senior year had been nothing like I had hoped or expected, but Ryan and I had made it through.

I put my head on his shoulder and we stared down at the lights of Nightshade. I didn't know everything that was ahead of me, but I knew I could face it with Ryan beside me.

Acknowledgments

A great many people worked to get the Dead Is series out into the world. So thanks to the bloggers, reviewers, librarians, fans, and friends who told one person to read this series! Thanks to all the hard-working people at Houghton Mifflin Harcourt, especially my wonderful editor Julie Tibbott, who managed to keep her sense of humor even when I went way off outline. My agent, Stephen Barbara, is sheer awesomeness, but everyone already knows that.

Thanks to my writer friends who keep me sane, read manuscripts at the drop of a hat, and are always up for coffee! And to my husband and children, who give me the gift of time to write.

Marlene Perez is the author of *The Comeback*, *Love in the Corner Pocket*, and the five books in the Dead Is series, including *Dead Is the New Black*, which was named an ALA Quick Pick for Reluctant Young Adult Readers. She lives in Orange County, California, with her family. She survived her Grad Night party, but just barely.

www.marleneperez.com